BOOKS BY BRYHER AVAILABLE
FROM PARIS PRESS

The Heart to Artemis: A Writer's Memoirs
The Player's Boy: A Novel
Visa for Avalon

OTHER NOVELS AND NON-FICTION BY BRYHER

Amy Lowell: A Critical Appreciation
Beowulf
Civilians
The Coin of Carthage
The Colors of Vaud
The Days of Mars: A Memoir, 1940-1946
Development and *Two Selves*
Film Problems of Soviet Russia
The Fourteenth of October
Gate to the Sea
Roman Wall
Ruan
This January Tale
West

THE PLAYER'S BOY

A Novel

THE

BRYHER

PLAYER'S BOY

INTRODUCTION BY *Patrick Gregory*

PARIS
PRESS
Ashfield, MA

First Paris Press edition, 2006.
The Player's Boy was published by Pantheon Books, Inc., 1953
and by Collins, London, 1957.

Paris Press is grateful for the generous support of the
Massachusetts Cultural Council, the Estate of W. Bryher, and the many
individuals and foundations that made the publication of this book possible.

Library of Congress Cataloging-in-Publication Data

Bryher, 1894-1983
The player's boy : a novel / Bryher ; with an introduction
by Patrick Gregory. -- 1st Paris Press ed.
p. cm.
ISBN-13: 978-1-930464-09-4 (pbk. : alk. paper)
ISBN-10: 1-930464-09-6 (pbk. : alk. paper)
1. Theater--England--History--16th century--Fiction.
2. London (England)--Fiction. I. Title.

PR6003.R98P57 2006
823'.914--dc22

2006009789

ACEGIJHFDB

Printed in the United States of America.

FOR

H.D.

It is but giving over of a game
that must be lost.

PHILASTER. *Act III. Scene 1.*

CONTENTS

.⸰~ᴗ᯽ᴖ~⸰.

Introduction

ETWEEN 1949 AND 1968 BRYHER published nine works of historical fiction. Begun in mid-life, this series of works marked a distinct departure from her earlier writings, and taken as a whole it constitutes her most enduring contribution to English letters.

The settings for the novels vary: from Italy in the 4th century B.C. to England during the Blitz, and each of these geographical locations marks a significant episode in the author's intellectual and emotional development. For example, *Coin of Carthage* grew out of her rapturous encounters with the Near East while traveling as a child with her father ("Nobody," she wrote in *The Heart to Artemis: A Writer's Memoirs,* "ever gets over their first camel"),[1] and *Ruan* harks back to her youthful discovery of Cornwall from which she was to draw her name, Bryher, while *The Colors of Vaud* is a belated homage to her adopted home canton in Switzerland. It is her deep personal attachment to these places that bestows on the books a particular air of authenticity.

All the novels are characterized by a concern for correct historical detail, as well as an almost uncanny sense of time and place. All depict a society in the throes of dissolution, caught up in a shift of values and beliefs imposed from both without and within. As an historian — and Bryher was an historian as well as a novelist — she understands that it does not always take a holocaust or total war to undo the fabric of daily living, that irreversible forces can be let loose by insidious changes in government and in culture. The chief figures in her novels are never the change-makers — the kings, tyrants, or power brokers who stalk the pages of most historical romances — but representatives of the common folk — the artisan, shopkeeper, farmwife, or laborer — who are forced to confront events essentially beyond their control. All the novels pose the question: How can individual integrity be sustained under such circumstances? The answers Bryher proposes are not always cheery.

The Player's Boy is the darkest and most personal of her novels. Darkest because its conclusion leaves so little room for maneuvering; most personal, because Bryher had since her adolescent years a very special affinity for Elizabethan London and because the underlying structure of the tale touches, if only indirectly, on intimate aspects of her own story. But before discussing these matters, let me briefly sketch the historical background against which the action of *The Player's Boy* takes place.

.·~૮ᏁᎧ~·.

The curtain rises on England in the year 1605. Queen Elizabeth has been dead for two years, Shakespeare is engaged in the composition of *Macbeth,* perhaps *King Lear,* the Gunpowder Plot is in its final conspiratorial stages, and the Stuarts have come to the throne in the person of James VI of Scotland, bringing with him a cohort of impoverished nobles, rapacious fortune hunters, and sketchy hangers-on. The king himself is intelligent, pragmatic, and devious in his dealings; and his habit of showering favors on handsome young courtiers of dubious distinctions adds a further element of ambivalence to a court already rife with personal and political intrigue. Underlying all is an ominous groundswell of religious fanaticism occasioned in part by the public's uncertainty about the king's own religious leanings and distrust of his behind-the-scenes dealings with Catholic Spain. A vague sense of decadence hangs in the air, along with a general feeling that the times are out of joint. As the young narrator of our novel explains, "We seemed to be suffering from some intermittent fever, not dangerous in itself, but able to spread a blight across our days, so that nothing seemed completely the right colour, and the only men left with zest were our enemies, the Puritans."[2]

The second half of the novel begins some thirteen years later with the execution of Sir Walter Ralegh. It is here that the scene darkens even more and the intermingling of history and fictional narrative grows more complex.

Statesman, visionary, man of action, author of a monumental History of the World and several lyric poems worthy of a great poetic era, Ralegh stands before the crowd as a towering relic of England's waning glory; and when he kneels to place his head on the block, the occasion suddenly assumes an aura of ritual impiety. Bryher recounts the onlookers' awed silence as they come to realize that they are witnessing the ignoble end of a glorious age.

At this halfway point of the novel the protagonist has grown from a boy to manhood; from a boy-actor carried away by his own rhapsodic utterances, he has now become a journeyman factor, struggling to wrest a living wage from an indifferent world — translated as it were from the poetry of youth to the prose of adulthood. The novel lays bare the painful process of the young hero's coming of age while hinting at corresponding shifts in the historical processes. "Time tangled, it never ran in a straight scythe cut, as they pretended in the moralities, but lay in loops, like grass at haying time when conies scampered for safety and stem and flower were upside down together."[3]

.·~ᝐ~·.

The geographical settings of her novels were, as I have suggested, of biographical significance to Bryher, and *The*

Player's Boy can be said to be her ultimate novel about London, where she spent a part of her childhood, and momentous interludes during the two world wars.

When World War II broke out Bryher had been a resident of Switzerland for well over a decade. In 1940, after the German air campaign against England was fully underway, she escaped from her home in Vevey and rejoined her friends in London. The itinerary through occupied France, Spain, and Portugal promised very real perils, but all her life Bryher had an inclination for risk-taking adventures. The prospect of danger only heightened her determination to make the trip, and she did.

In 1944 she finished a novel recounting the trials of two women teashop proprietors during the Blitz (published some years later under the title of *Beowulf*). But the ruins of London, with their multiple levels of history exposed to the sky, continued to haunt her. As a novelist she felt a need to revisit the city. By placing this second literary visitation several centuries back in time, she found the proper perspective from which to exercise her gifts as a storyteller and student of the past. In choosing the twilight of the Age of Elizabeth she was linking it to an historical period that held a privileged place in her literary imagination.

In her memoir *Days of Mars,* Bryher describes attending an open-air performance of *As You Like It* in Regent's Park during the war:

I suppose by now I had really learned a great deal about the period and often muttered Elizabethan to myself. . . . Now suddenly the wit of the comedy gripped me. I laughed as I had never laughed in any theatre before or since. "It's so funny," I tried to explain to my astonished neighbour, who had not, apparently, understood a single one of the jokes. All that had happened was that I had read Elizabethan intensely and continually and was seeing the play among what could have been an original audience of apple-sellers and citizens. Do not mistake me, I had not slipped back in time although for a moment I almost felt I had; it was because the conditions of the afternoon could not have been very different from Shakespeare's time; we faced the ending of an age, the slowing down of a great period of expansion and exploration and this brought with it a fear of the future.[4]

That fear pervades the novel, growing in intensity as the tale progresses. It is accompanied by a profound sense of loss, a gradual draining away of innocence and idealism, and the emergence of a harsh new urban sophistication replacing the age-old pastoral traditions of England's past.

·~ᴄᴊᴑ~·

If the time and geography of *The Player's Boy* had special biographical significance to Bryher, so too did certain elements of the story. She stated:

There are times when destiny puts the right book in the hands of an apprentice. I discovered, prowling among the books in my father's library when I was fifteen, Hazlitt's *The Dramatic Literature of the Age of Elizabeth*. It was there I found Bellario, Philaster's page. Nobody told me that a girl's part on the Elizabethan stage had been played by a boy. I learned her speeches and quoted them during the stresses of school.[5]

James Sands, the player's boy of the novel, assumes the role of Bellario in the opening performance of Beaumont and Fletcher's *Philaster*. Like the youthful Bryher he is transported by the language; the role becomes the high point of his stage career. Allusions to the play can be found throughout the novel — most conspicuously in the quotation that serves as a heading for the final chapter.[6] One need not know the play to grasp what Bryher is up to in the novel, but since *Philaster* serves as a sort of palimpsest to the work, it is worthwhile pausing to review the plot.

Philaster, the deposed heir to the kingdom of Sicily, is in love with Arethusa, daughter of the usurping king, who returns his affections. The king, in order to strengthen his hold on his restless subjects (many of whom remain loyal to the young prince Philaster) arranges to marry off his daughter to a Spanish duke and thus effect a military alliance with Spain. Euphrasia, daughter of one of the king's courtiers, is also in love with Philaster. She recognizes the futility of her suit, and disguising herself as a boy under the name of Bellario manages to attach herself to Philaster as his page. In order to have a go-between to convey messages to and from his beloved, Philaster bequeaths his page to Arethusa. Thus we have: Philaster who loves Arethusa, Arethusa who loves Philaster, and Euphrasia/Bellario who loves Philaster and who is obliged to serve them both until the play's denouement.

The resolution is peculiar, even for a romantic drama of the time. The Spanish suitor is exposed as a poltroon, and the good people of the kingdom rise up to depose their king, who at the last moment, manages to strike a deal: Philaster, the king proclaims, is to marry his daughter and be designated as heir-apparent to the throne. Upon this announcement, Bellario throws off her disguise, declares that she will never marry, and asks permission to serve both prince and princess as their devoted attendant. Turning to her betrothed, the princess declares, "I, Philaster, / Cannot be jealous though you had a lady / Drest like a page to serve you; nor will I / Suspect her living here." Then, addressing herself to the former Bellario, she offers these words of welcome: "Come, live with me; / Live free as I do. She that loves my lord, / Cursed be the wife that hates her!" And so the curtain descends on the happy — or resolute — ménage à trois.

The Player's Boy is dedicated to the poet H.D. (Hilda Doolittle) and anyone aware of the conjugal complexities that marked the long-term relationship between the two women may wish to ruminate on the pathos and gentle wit contained in the inscription.[7]

.·~ᴄ⚮ᴐ~·.

The fifty years between 1590 and the declaration of the Commonwealth in 1640 was the Golden Age of English poetry. For the most part this poetry was written for the theater and declaimed to enthusiastic, vociferous, and critically discriminating audiences who thronged a handful of playhouses on both sides of the Thames.[8] A host of dramatic authors including Shakespeare, Marlowe, Jonson, Middleton, Beaumont, Fletcher, Webster, and Tourneur produced amongst them a body of work for the theater that remains unsurpassed for its emotional intensity and range of lyrical expression.

The Player's Boy is perhaps the best fictional evocation of the Elizabethan theatrical scene that we possess. Bryher's lifelong fascination with the time and place, her loving concern with the minutiae of Elizabethan daily living, have been put to good use. Her instincts as a novelist lead her to make her young hero Sands something less than a natural performer — unlike his rival player boy, Dicky, who effortlessly compels the rapt attention of the crowd. Sands' hesitations and gaucheries allow Bryher to describe the arduous training involved in bringing about a service-able performance. (Bryher herself played a small support-ing role in *Borderline,* an avant-garde film of the late 1920s directed by her husband Kenneth Macpherson and starring Paul Robeson. The experience was probably chastening, con-tributing to her regard for the exigencies of the actor's craft.)

Dryden, in his *Of Dramatick Poesie, an Essay,* writes: "I am apt to believe that the English Language in [Beaumont and Fletcher] arrived at its highest perfect; what words have since been taken in are rather superfluous than ornamental."[9] Bryher, I feel, would have concurred. As a writer of English prose, Bryher considered herself committed to the modernist movement, and looked to America and the Continent for models (she had particular respect for the writings of Gide and Hesse, and in her last years was much taken by the pro-ponents of the *nouveau roman*). Her ear, however, remained Elizabethan. There are few superfluities in her language. Her writing is lucid, direct and compact, and in her fiction she shows herself a disciplined and meticulous stylist. To read-ers of today, accustomed to the overwrought metaphors and intricate imagery that characterizes the work of many of our most esteemed contemporary novelists, her prose may seem lacking in flash. But she is one of those rare novelists who stand up well to rereading. Her sentences are remarkable not for their complexity but for their concision. Her descriptive passages of people or landscapes are always precisely framed and in sharp focus, and reward the reader with the same freshness of vision that one experiences on viewing the photographs of an André Kertész or a Berenice Abbott.

The writing of *The Player's Boy* presented a particular challenge to its author: how to capture the flavor and ambience of the time without reverting to a pastiche of the Elizabethan language? It's a problem familiar to all historical novelists — easily enough solved if the period is sufficiently remote and the language foreign — but tricky if one is dealing with one's own native tongue. And doubly tricky for Bryher, for whom Elizabethan was almost a second language. There is in the dialogue a subtle strangeness, a slight brogue or tang, that evokes the flavor of Elizabethan speech without descending into imitation — sometimes effected by the use of an uncommon word in a familiar context. It is here that Bryher's restraint, taste, and fine ear carry the day, and her overall resolution of the problem constitutes a stylistic tour de force.

⁓ↂ⁓

The conclusion of *The Player's Boy* comes as a slap in the face, but it has been deeply foreshadowed and the reader submits to its inevitability. Certainly it reflects the author's response to what she sees as the growing coarseness and degradation of society. Bryher is too conscientious an historian to draw direct parallels between the past and present; every age has its own distinctive shape and colors. Yet turning from the past to address the present, her voice does occasionally take on a tone of prophetic admonition, touched with bitter irony. In her later years, she would write:

> Never expect morality or justice to succeed; it is the parasites who win riches and a comfortable old age, seldom the worthy citizens. Scheme, wriggle, and bargain but beware of telling the truth and above all, never be a hero. It is an unwise affectation, particularly after a war.[10]

A bleak message indeed. Yet the reader may find some room for hope in Bryher's use of the words "expect" and "seldom," and in the fact that she continued to write novels well into old age that extol the transcendent virtues of loyalty, courage, and personal integrity. In times such as ours it is well that readers rid themselves of a need for the obligatory happy endings that mar so much of our contemporary fiction, keeping in mind that the usefulness of both history and fiction lies in their commitment to truth — factual and figurative — and what they have to tell us about the vagaries of the human condition.

— *Patrick Gregory*

Notes

1 Bryher, *The Heart to Artemis* (Ashfield, MA: Paris Press, Inc. 2006), p. 67.

2 Bryher, *The Player's Boy* (Ashfield, MA: Paris Press, Inc. 2006), pp. 76-77.

3 Ibid., p. 178.

4 Bryher, *The Days of Mars* (New York: Harcourt Brace Jovanovich, Inc. 1972), p. 152.

5 Ibid., p. 100.

6 "*Phi.* Oh, but thou dost not know
   What 'tis to die.
   Bel. Yes, I do know, my lord:
      'Tis less than to be born; a lasting sleep;
      A quiet resting from all jealousy,
      A thing we all pursue; I know besides,
      It is but giving over of a game
      That must be lost." Beaumont and Fletcher, *Philaster or Love Lies A-Bleeding*, Act III, Scene 1.

7 Bryher's marriage to H.D.'s lover Kenneth Macpherson and the trio's subsequent life-long friendship is surely an example of Philasterian triangularity.

8   Under Cromwell the playhouses were shut down, not to be
    reopened until the restoration of the royalty in 1660, at which
    time women began to assume the female parts onstage, thus
    bringing an end to the traditional role of boy actors.

9   John Dryden, *Of Dramatick Poesie* (Oxford: Oxford University
    Press, 1964), p. 89.

10 Bryher, *The Days of Mars* (New York: Harcourt Brace Jovanovich,
    Inc. 1972), p. 165.

THE PLAYER'S BOY

I

Mouse-coloured Velvet.

"I give to Samuell Gilborne my late apprentice the somme of xl^s and my mouse coulloured velvet hose and a white taffity doublet a black taffity suite my purple cloake sworde and dagger And my base vyoll Item I give to James Sands my apprentice the somme of xl^s And a citterne and a Bandore and a Lute to be paide and delivered unto him at th' expiracon of his terme of yeares in his Indenture of apprentishoode."

Will of Augustine Phillips,
May 4^{th,} 1605.

May 1ˢᵗ, 1605.

ASTER AWSTEN was lying in a great bed with painted hangings. He did not hear me steal into the room. His eyes were open, but the light had gone from them; there was neither repose nor gaiety in his face, only fear.

Outside was May, the fresh grass and the bramble, but this chamber reeked of strange apothecary smells, "fever scents" old Mistress Crofton called them, who would never wait for a wherry at low water on Bank End without holding lavender or a posy to her nose. I stood, trying to smile, to hold my face that he might not notice how shocked I was; when we had parted so short a while before, he had been radiantly alive.

"Master Awsten," I whispered at last, "how do you?"

"What dost thou want here, Sands?" He turned his head

with such difficulty, and his body under the sheets was so death-like and rigid that I shuddered. "Thou shouldst not see thy master like this. But then I am not thy master any longer," he murmured bitterly.

"You will be my master always." I knelt in front of him, before the drawn-back curtains. "Ever since Edmund brought us news that you were sick of a spring fever, I have waited for this holiday to come to you."

"A spring fever! Spring is over for me. But come nearer to me, boy, it's not the plague, I've lain here too long for that. . . ." and as I took a little stool to sit by him, I heard him mutter, "Would it had been the plague, it would now be ended." Then he began to cough, and I held a cup of cordial to his lips.

It was a terrible sound on this first of May morning, when mummers were dancing in the fields, and the surliest constable wore a favour in his cap, and as the fit ceased he dropped back on to his pillow again, with his eyes closed, and a face so pale, that I wondered if he were already dying. It was not his soul, he was too weary, but the blood in him that fought for life. Why did this have to happen to Awsten of all men, he who had given so much to us; if he had to die, why could it not be swiftly, without suffering, as I had once seen a man die in single fight, with a sword thrust through his body?

"Will you come to the May?" A child's voice rose lightly

from the garden, it was one of his daughters, Maudlyne perhaps or Anne. I had noticed them as I had entered the courtyard, stepping in a round, with favours in their hair, the elder teaching the younger, and the baby of them all breaking off the game to sit on the grass and dig its heels into the daisies. In less than a fortnight the first roses would be out. Awsten stirred, his eyes opened again, and he managed to whisper, "Come, Sands, what news?"

"We miss you, all of us have missed you ever since you left us. I heard Master Armin say a week ago, 'The great days are over.' Oh, if you could only come back to us...." I thought of the unearthly beauty of his last jigge, when even the vainest gallant had not moved his chair, and for five full minutes jealousy and the newest favourite had been forgotten, because we had been rapt above hunger and misery and common danger into the sphere of fire, where Awsten, their messenger, had danced with the spirits in pure, unthreatened joy. "They say Fire left no place in you for any of the moist humours; you are all flame."

The words seemed to bring a trace of joy back to his face. "Dare I venture to say now, Sands, a carcass on a sick bed, that it will be a long time before you find another Awsten to amuse you, without Sir Preacher reproving me for pride? What were the words in that sermon? 'Certain arrogant men who, because they have put on the semblance of a king, think that they are royal ...'" He whined the words in so perfect a

4

mockery of old Dr Bentwood that I had to laugh out loud; then Awsten's eyes wandered to the figures painted on the arras, and he muttered, "So much to hear, so much to know, why can't they find a way to fight this fever?"

"Fevers take a long time; my grandfather lay sick of an ague for three months, but he played Jack o' the Green with the best of them the next feast day."

"Did he so? Did he so? Ah, Sands, why should I rebel, yet I do rebel; nothing, not all the wishes of my friends, not all the glory, will give me back what thou in thine innocence dost not even know that thou hast, and that is youth."

"And I would give it to you gladly. It's an unhappy time." I remembered Mother Crofton's words when Awsten had first taken me, "Sell the silly child, he'll be no good to you. The drop of a feather frightens him."

Awsten seemed not to hear me but went on, "Nothing I want can I have, and I can have everything I want... except life."

I ventured to take his hand, it was not burning as I had expected but cold, moist and heavy as if the ocean were in it. "Master Awsten, fear not, the fever is lower, you will soon be strong again."

He shook his head. "I wanted arras, boy, I wanted velvet. Here are my hangings; I gave the Flemish merchant twenty nobles for them, and what use are they to me now? They mock me lying here." His eyes were fixed on the centre of the panel, on the grave figure of the young Apollo that his hands were too weak to touch. "Still frightened, Sands?" He seemed to be reading my thoughts. "Thou hast it easy. Gentle thou mayst not be, but thy training is the envy of any courtier's child. Thou art a royal apprentice with the King's colours on thy cap and I, though I was a gentleman's son, slept my boyhood out under the open sky. That's where I bred this fever. The times I lay in a ditch, or in the flea-ridden straw of an old barn, and dreamed of arras! But the dawns, boy, the singing of the thrushes, the grey in the sky to tell our cold limbs that presently the sun would shine again, they all come back to me, lying here, who never dreamed that I should miss them."

There had always been much gossip about Master Awsten's birth. Some said that he was a drover's son, and that that was why he had the itch of movement in him; others, that his mother had been a waiting gentlewoman whom the lord of the manor had surprised in the arms of his son, one sleepy July evening. Awsten himself pretended that he had first emerged from a giant pie at the banquet of the Shoemakers' Company, babbling to the citizens, "A merry evening, sweet gentlemen." If anyone questioned him further, Awsten would look up with such a power of frozen anger in his face that the fellow would break his sentence off before he had completed it. Certainly Awsten had never learned to act the courtier; he was one.

"Yes, boy, thou art taught fencing and singing, to speak and play the lute; what wouldst thou learn more at the Inns of Court, unless it were a scrap of Latin that never won a man, as far as I could see, a flagon of wine to set before his meat? I followed my master the length and breadth of England, with a flower stuck bravely in my cap to conceal that we wore no nobleman's livery, hoping some justice or other would give us leave to tumble at a fair. I've been whipped and set in the stocks with my master sitting supperless beside me, and had to bear his anger afterwards. Dost know what it feels like to come breakfastless to a farm, and before you can ask the milkmaid, with a pretty compliment, to pour a drop of buttermilk into your cup, have a hulking churl set a great mastiff on you as if you were some wretched cur at a bull baiting, flung into the ring to be rid of it? No, Sands, thou dreamer, what dost thou know of these things? I've heard thee complaining about Southwark, it's too gross for thy fine nostrils, but it's a kindlier place than most villages. Thou wilt never be like thy master, boy, I danced a Kemp's Morris, day in and day out, not for my supper but my life." His face had the downcast pallor of the disinherited son at the beginning of an interlude, and his eyes closed wearily.

"I tried to do your bidding," I said, the tears already in my eyes. I was always laughed at for being what they called lily-livered, yet how could I help minding the misery and filth? It was frightening to see some young fellow who had been snapping his heels in a crosscut caper only an hour before, lying dead on the stones after a stupid quarrel, and if I shivered when the plague bell tolled, wasn't this natural after my father had died of it? Other youths were just as terrified as I was, but somehow they were able to disguise their feelings more, or to wriggle their way out with a jest, if a man called them queasy. Words never came easily to me; I could look and feel, but not speak.

"Forget my ramblings, Sands," Awsten noticed that I was crying, "thou hast been a good boy, as obedient an apprentice as I ever had. And confidence will come with growth." Then he began to cough again, and old goodwife Doggett entered with a tray. "Is the boy tiring you, Master?" She looked at me reprovingly. "Make your legge and go."

"Let him stay; with this pestilential cough of mine, I've had no chance to talk to him as yet, and he must carry word from me to my fellows."

Mistress Doggett eyed me suspiciously, but I stood with my cap in my hand —, my eyes to the floor, without saying a syllable. "The leech said you were to have no visitors," she protested.

"Visitors, yes, but Sands is my own boy. He can wait whilst I drink that posset of yours, and then I'll send him to the kitchen. And see that he has plenty to eat before he begins his journey. He has given up his holiday to come to me."

"That limp's a worse sound for a sick man than any London news," Master Awsten grumbled, as we listened to the old woman struggling down the stairs. "There's ague in it and rheumatism, and what good has the leech ever done her, what can he do to help this decaying of the body, against which there are neither elixirs nor charms. Or are there?" I looked up in such amazement that Awsten smiled. "Open that cupboard, and thou wilt find some Rhenish wine. My neighbour brought it yesterday, and I still had wit enough to make him hide it. For five days I have swallowed their potions and done their bidding — it has only made me worse. Here, throw this stuff out of the casement," he pushed the cordial towards me, "and give me something to drink."

I hesitated, and he looked up with the old command in his face. "Thou art still my boy, Sands, fill my glass." The emperor was dying on his throne in the fifth act; I bowed as he had taught me, and served him on my knee.

"*Rubies dissolve but not my smarting thoughts,*" he murmured, as if he recognised what I did. "But memories, child, these burn; did no ballad monger tell thee of the shirt of Nessus?

*'The sweeter the spring
the worse the nettles sting.'*

It may be a country proverb, as they say, but it is truer than

9

your townsman's wit." He gulped the Rhenish eagerly, and handed me the empty glass to be refilled.

"That was the time I was in love with Maudlyne. Her father was the owner of the *Swan*. She had freckles on her nose, and her eyes were like those blue flowers that brighten all the meadows in the spring, and have a different name in every shire. I wanted to buy her a ribbon, but I never had a groat in my hand of my own. That year the plague was bad, no theatres could open after Lent, and they stopped many of the fairs. People were so stupidly afraid that it was easier to die of hunger than the pest. My master had a friend, the captain of a barge sailing to the Low Countries, with a cargo of osier baskets to be used for storing fish. This fellow took us aboard, and I stood on deck most of the first night, as moon-sick as a calf, fretting because Maudlyne had been sent to her uncle at Brentford to keep her away from the infection, and I was sure that I should never see her little snub nose again. And the sail swung round in a gust of wind and almost knocked me into the Thames. How the sailors laughed! It was the only time for weeks that I had had food enough in my belly, and first I was too love-sick and then too sea-sick to enjoy it. Lord, Lord, the foolishness of youth! I tossed about on my straw pallet, and my master thought that I had taken the fever, until the captain came and looked at me. 'Why, the boy's green,' he laughed, 'it's Neptune's sickness, the winds will blow it out of him.' But they never did, I lay there, and groaned till we anchored."

"But how could you play in Flanders if they speak no English?"

"English! I was a tumbling boy and you can jigge in any language. Some players we knew had gone out the summer before, and had much praised the country. We walked and jigged and earned a penny for our meat here, and a ride in an old cart there, until by the end of May we were almost in the middle of Germany. Then we stopped in an old town whose count gave us leave to go to all the neighbouring fairs. It was hot and flat, but there were cherry trees in the burghers' gardens, the sweetest fruit I ever tasted, and a dull, shimmering red, like the sloping roofs of their houses. Nobody ever refused me a cap full if I wanted them; they were as different from our Kentish whitehearts as a goose is from a sparrow. Of course the people laughed at our attempts to get our tongues round their words, the simplest things had names as long as a fathom of twisting eel, but never believe, Sands, that foreigners are monsters. They set no dogs on us, although we wore no livery."

"And how long were you in Germany?" I leaned forward as if I were watching a play, forgetting the smell of camphor, and the gaunt, mask-like face. There was a road beyond these bed curtains, and it led to a yard full of geese, where two girls were handing eggs up to a boy astride a wall, while the old farmer drowsed on a bench, with his hands folded in his lap. He was dressed in the same wide breeches that the Dutch captains wore. I had seen them when they landed from the barges at Queenhythe.

"A summer, a single summer. I slept with two stable boys in a garret above the cobbled square, and sultry nights when even the Watch was asleep I climbed out on a ledge and sat there, looking at the stars. Their sky is deeper than it is with us, a real gallant's velvet. And I used to sing,

'*Though it be May,*
Leave the sweet rushes,
Crush, if you will, the hay
But leave the rushes
For us this single day
To meet and play...'

and wonder if Maudlyne were true to me. Don't smile, Sands." But I was not smiling, I was simply looking at him eagerly. "After thou hast fallen in love thyself, thou wilt understand."

"I shall fall in love with the Muses," I said with uncommon firmness, looking up at the arras.

"Go to, boy, go to; they're cold." Awsten stirred almost merrily, the pillows slipped, and I leaned over and straightened them. "Find thyself a mortal when the time comes, and now give me some more wine." I hesitated, and he looked at me with that curious, proud look he had had when he played the emperor Sardanapalus. "What does it matter whether I die now, or come Sunday. Perhaps this is the last time I shall be happy."

Happy! Happy with me! I felt as if I had drunk up all the wine that was still left in the silver flagon, but I made myself sit quietly, not daring to move, lest Mistress Doggett should hear and call me down to the kitchen, whilst Master Awsten drained his glass, and a flush of colour came gradually back to his cheeks.

"Yes," he continued, "we were in a strange land, but they laughed. That was where I learned my art, boy; there were none of your asides, and your Prologue saying, 'Listen, here comes Master Goodventure unexpectedly back from his journey.' I did not know their tongue, nor they mine, and I had to make them hear Master Goodventure cloppering up the steps in a fury, while I gave fair Alice a last kiss, and leapt out of the casement.

'Kiss me, Alice, let me go.'"

He has the fever again, I thought, for this was an old song that serving maids had hummed before I was out of my cradle. I wanted to take away the cup, but he shook his head, and let it fall idly on the coverlet.

"I showed them Master Goodventure turning out the closet and finding nothing, no, not even a little wooden dagger; and then they had to see his face, and how they laughed when he ran out and back and down into the cellar where the wind — or Alice — clapped the door shut on him. Then I danced my triumph under her window, as if Jack or Tom or whatever name you want to give a youth had nothing else to do but catch the stars and make love."

"Oh, that's the jigge you chose the night you said farewell to us! We wondered why you wanted an out-of-fashion ballad instead of a new play — till you began." In Awsten's hands the common interlude of girl, lover and elderly husband was transformed into a conflict between light and darkness, where beauty fled from the world's net that would have caged and destroyed her.

"Didst like it, boy?" Awsten's smile was the benediction of the Muses. "I had to remember it one last time myself." Again he held the glass out to be filled.

"Fortune always gives us one summer for a garland, to encourage us, I suppose, and delude us into thinking that if we are good we shall be happy. I can see that market square now, as if I were standing on its cobbles again, with my master playing his fife, and a rose in my cap to remind me of the Queen, and little did I dream then that I should ever wear her colours. As long as the people laughed there were no beatings, but a good supper afterwards, sometimes even praise. That meant more to me than the fat capon that a gentleman sent in to us one evening. I had the foolish notion that Maudlyne might be proud of me. Then the apples ripened, and so, if we wanted to play in the Christmas revels, it was time to go home. The day before we left, when nobody was looking, the lord of the castle slipped a piece of silver into my hand, and I bought the ribbon for Maudlyne after all.

"At first we tramped through open country, while the leaves shortened into golden frills on the birch trees above us, but before we could cross the Dutch border it had turned to rain, and we were thankful to find our captain friend back from another voyage and waiting in the harbour for the right wind. I was just as sick on my way back as I had been going over, and I shall never forget how the great cobble stones wavered and swayed when we landed, as if I were paddling down a stream instead of walking on solid ground. The first Sunday after we got to London I took my ribbon and went off to the *Swan*. There I found Maudlyne on a settle in front of the fire, with a great fellow almost out of his time sitting beside her. I knew then that all my summer singing and sighing had been wasted.

> *'Oh, ask not Margaret to stay,*
> *She'll never miss you,'"*

Awsten could only whisper the old catch,

> *"'But ask instead for Flemish Kate,*
> *She'll bring you ale, and gladly kiss you.'"*

He was tired now, and coughing again so loudly that I expected Mistress Doggett to hear him, and come clattering up the stairs. The air was grim and stale, and I noticed a stain on the arras, just above Apollo's lute. The may had begun to flower under the window (but the wall was between us), a navigator's map of stars in the green, dark hedge. I took a cloth and wiped Awsten's forehead, and even forced a little of the cordial he detested between his lips. What did it profit Dame Fortune to shower him with so many gifts, if just as they were opening into a great, perfect rose, she snatched them away? Of what use was any beginning, if this were the inevitable end? Perhaps Awsten read my thoughts, because he managed to whisper, "Courage, Sands, thou hast youth." I shook my head, and he looked up at me reproachfully, with that cold glance that had always been more successful than a dozen oaths in stilling our idle chatter when he was studying a new speech. "Wake up, boy, the glass runs swiftly, and no dreaming will help thee. Master Sly was younger than thou art when he came to me as my first pupil, but we were more like older and younger brothers than prentice and master. The Canary we swallowed! The reckonings we never paid! There was more impudence in the way that he tucked his cap under his arm than thou hast in thy whole body! I know not what has happened to this age! Life is an adventure, not a patient crawling from swaddling bands to grave clothes. When you lie in a bed that you will never leave, as I do now, it won't be fantasies that will come to you; no, you'll think of the night that you slipped over Justice Bradford's wall to fill your wallet with his choicest pears, or the evening you surprised Kate milking behind the barn, and kissed her. We never hung our heads wondering if the morrow would bring us shelter, we leapt 'like pards' upon the moment. Yes, I have had the sweet, and now I must taste the hemlock, as your playwriting fellows call it. I am face to face with my only enemy" (and I knew that he meant death), "he has flicked his rapier at me a hundred times, and I have jigged over the housetops as if he were an old, slippered man. Now here he is with a new trick of tierce, and there is no running away from him in this narrow room. Who wants to live with a fire in the chest, and this ever growing feebleness? I don't want to be old, Sands, I'll laugh at him when he is ready for me; yet, oh, the things I could do, the way I could shatter your hearts, if one week, one single week of thy youthfulness were granted to me!"

"Take it," I sobbed, "it means nothing to me, it is easier to die than to be alive."

"For shame, Sands, those were thy words the first time that I met thee. Dost thou not like the touch of silk and the taste of a good pasty? Or to watch a swan come proudly down the river?"

"They are only a few moments in a great sea of suffering."

"Art ailing too, boy, or is it lack of growth? I had rather that my pence were stolen and that thou filched my wine, as thy fellow prentices do, it would make a better man of thee, and yet, my little changeling, I am glad to have thee now, sitting here beside me."

I moved my stool nearer, and he closed his eyes. The wine had made him drowsy, and his breath came in heavy gasps, while his arms lay flabbily on the coverlet. Still, I was glad that he could sleep, even if it were only for a moment. Perhaps his venturing youth would return to comfort him, the ragged flowers, the bells of a lost morris jingling through the wood. Yet as I imagined this, I felt a heaviness in the air, as if Fate and not Mistress Doggett were waiting in the chamber below. I began to shiver myself, and when a movement of Awsten's body sent the flagon rolling to the floor, I was too desolate, too lonely, to stretch my hand out and pick it up.

Nobody could ever replace Awsten. It was almost three years since he had found me in neighbour Mitcham's orchard, on a hot summer day. The village boys teased me, and the ploughman sent me errands, so as soon as I had heard voices I had ducked behind some bushes into a hiding place that I had contrived, and peeped between the leaves. "There ought to be a path here," a man had grumbled, and the footsteps had ceased. Strangers frequently took the path that ran beside Goodman Lockyer's cottage, thinking that it was a short cut to the highway, when instead it stopped at our gate. "Let's rest a moment," another voice had replied, deep, clear, and so beautiful that I had forgotten my fears, and scrambled up from my seat.

All that I had seen at first had been a tall figure, some gallant surely, for he wore a doublet of the newest knot pattern, and a fresh, white ruff. His riding cap had dangled from his fingers, and as I had approached them, his hair had reminded me of a rose noble, it was such fine gold. He had already swung himself up to the flat stone on the top of the low wall and sat there, very comfortably, looking at Lockyer's fat cows that were busily chewing the pasture.

> *"A year ago, a year ago,*
> *my love swore she was true,*
> *the bumpy lambs played in the grass,*
> *the hedge was brave and new."*

It was a silly song, the stable boys had been whistling it all summer, but he had sung it differently, as if he really wanted a girl to come lazily across the field.

"If we are to reach London before nightfall, Master Phillips, we had better walk back to the road instead of loitering here," the second, shorter man had protested.

"Time enough, time enough, I was country bred myself, remember, and this reminds me of the hours I looked round the hedges for the herb they call bread and cheese. Often enough it was the only breakfast I had."

Oh, I had thought at once, you must be a younger son. Then I had noticed the silver hilt of his sword, perhaps he had been overseas, and made his fortune fighting against the Turks?

"Sirs," I had said, forgetting my usual shyness, "there's a path to the village, if you will cross the orchard."

"And whose child art thou, come to save us from tramping half a mile in this midsummer heat; is this thy father's land?"

"No," I had shaken my head, "my father lives in Southwark, but after my mother died last March, he sent me to my godparents for the summer."

The tall man had searched his pocket for a coin, I had seen it in his hand, and it was silver. "Here's something for thy courtesy, to buy a cake of gingerbread next market."

I had looked up; even today I could not think how such boldness came to me. "I would rather hear you sing again than buy a cake."

"Bless the child, he knows what he wants," they had roared with laughter. "But it costs a sixpence to hear Master Phillips sing," the shorter fellow had teased me. "He is one of Her Majesty's players."

"Then I will take the coin and give it back to him for a song," I had protested and, abashed at my own impudence, was about to run away.

Master Awsten had caught me gently by the arm. "Art happy, boy, in these green meadows?"

"No," I had answered wonderingly, "how could I be?"

Something must have happened to make me unlike the other children, though I did not know what it was. I had even asked my mother if I could have been washed ashore at a shipwreck, and had got a clout on my head for my pains. The things that I longed for made my fellows laugh, and I disliked what they wanted. I was only a burden to my godparents; they called me a dull, moping lad, and try as I would, I could not please them.

The players had looked at me in silence, and Master Awsten had patted my head. "He has been beaten," he had murmured, "I know. But believe me, boy, gingerbread is a wonderful salve for aches."

"No," I had protested, because I wanted to be just, "I have only been beaten when I deserved it, but I am to be bound to a master come Michaelmas, and then I shall be shut up in a room, and never roam the meadows here again."

"And what wouldst thou like to do thyself?"

"Sometimes I have thought I should like to live alone in a wood, but then the snows would come, and it would be lonely."

"And what is thy name?" Master Awsten commanded.

"James Sands."

"No, changeling Sands," and he had smiled at me, just as I had seen him smile at his daughters later when they played with him. "Queen Mab must have forgotten thee after one of her dances. Hast thou ever been to a play?"

"Oh yes," I had answered eagerly, "it was the bravest

thing I ever saw, in a great courtyard with trumpeters, and the emperor died in it, most nobly."

How they had laughed! "And what wouldst thou say, young Sands, to being an emperor's page?" Awsten had asked the question gravely, like a councillor.

I had looked ashamed, thinking that they mocked me. Then Awsten had laughed so gaily that I had had to smile too, and his companion had murmured, "It's as likely a child as any other." I had led them to the village where their man was waiting with the horses, and they had sung, or whistled songs and catches all the way, or questioned me as to what my father did, and where he dwelt in Southwark. "We shall soon meet again," Master Awsten had said before he mounted, "and next time it will be thy turn to sing." I had not understood what he meant, until a message came for me a few days later, to return to my father in London. The day after my arrival I had been bound apprentice to Master Phillips.

There were footsteps in the courtyard below us, and Master Awsten stirred out of his doze. "Sir," I said timidly, lest Mistress Doggett were at hand to disturb us, "I was remembering the day we met. I beseech you, pardon me my stubbornness and negligence. No boy ever had a better master."

"The first days are hard. And I, through sickness, have been less than patient. Besides, what have I to scold thee for, except that thou changest from one shape to another, dreaming and mooning, when thou shouldst have thy feet upon the earth."

I hung my head, because this was true. Somehow whenever I should have been learning my notes, or practising a trick of fence, a wonderful strange butterfly of an idea would come, and I would follow it dreamily, whilst my fellows were busy with their work. I could see the shape of the sound, or the movement, high in air, but when it came to doing it myself, the note was false or my fingers clumsy.

"Thou hast more understanding, boy, than many of the others, but knowledge alone will never breed success unless it is paired with action. Though Fate is more to blame than thou art; first thy mother died, and then thy father, and now," he looked at me most sadly, "thine indentures are not half over, and I have to pass thee on to Master Sly."

"What do we do on the first of May,"

the children had begun another round,

"we pick you a posy before it is day."

I wanted to shout to them to stop, but Awsten continued, perhaps he did not hear them, "Greet my fellows, Sands, I miss them sadly, but do not tell them too much about this fever, it will pass."

"The summer is before us," I murmured; when I had

walked up from the river bank that morning, the coltsfeet and ragged robin had been as high as my knees.

"I'll get well, I'll sit under my apricocks like any cozener turned worthy merchant."

"Master Hodge has a violet cordial, they say, that brings much comfort."

"A violet cordial! Sands, am I a love-sick maid! There is only one cordial for a man, and that is a sup of burnt sack, with or without sugar."

I had to laugh; I had heard him jest like this a dozen times, stamping across the tavern floor until the flagons rang on their shelves, and the innkeeper hurried out, expecting to meet a young heir with the country mud still on his boots and the Inns of Court before him.

"Dame Fortune wants to show me she is still my mistress, but after she has chastened me enough, she will charm away these shiverings in a night. And Dr Carp will pretend it is his doing! Were you there the time I tottered up the steps to Alice in my black furred gown," memory made his voice a little stronger, "didst see me send the husband to the apothecary for a muscat pill, and as soon as the worthy fool had shut the door, drop my cloak, to stand before her in my peach-coloured satin?"

"How the people laughed!" Awsten, who was about to die, was acting that he was going to live, and almost making me believe him. "Yet it was your last jigge that I liked best, I wanted to cry out with the pain of it, it was not mortal."

"But it was no tragedy, boy, it was light, wanton stuff."

"As the gods conceive it," and I looked up at the Muses.

"There was one gesture that was never right," Awsten murmured thoughtfully.

"It was the perfection of perfection." Even from the outside row where I had stood with my fellow prentices, he had lifted us into the sky to tread in a golden globe, where neither Fate nor fear could touch us.

Awsten shook his head. "That was because thou didst not know what I wanted to do," he whispered, "I knew, only I can judge."

"Or Apollo." I pointed to the arras, and he smiled.

"Most of them never even saw what I was offering them, and then they called me proud!"

"It was you who showed us heaven, not Dr Bentwood with his sermons."

Awsten put his hand on mine; it was hot now, the fever was rising. "Thou art the gentlest boy I ever had, and loyal too. Sly first, then Gilborne; the company gave one its fellowship and trusted the other, after they were grown. Nobody can say that I did not look to the three of you, as if you had been my sons; but Sands, thou dreamer, wake up!"

It was no real reproof, for he smiled gratefully as I wrung out the cloth in fresh water and tried to cool his head. The children had run to the other side of the garden; all we heard now was the humming of the bees, and occasionally a distant voice. How meaningless this May Day splendour seemed, in front of Awsten's pain! I offered him the cordial again, but he pushed it away. "Gilborne shall have my last suit with the white taffety doublet," he murmured, turning his face away from the light. "We used to tell him that rather than show himself in frieze and straw, if he had to play Tom o' Bedlam, he would run away. How brave he will look in the mouse-coloured hose! He is a headstrong fellow, but all grace."

"Not the mouse-coloured velvet!" I half rose from the stool. Awsten had worn it once, to speak the epilogue that final evening, and I had seen, not taffeta, but the cold glory of the stars.

"Why, Sands, it is too big for thee. Thou wilt have to grow another foot to step into my hose."

"I do not want to wear it. It reminds me of the day you left me, and passed me on to Master Sly."

"And is he not good to thee, boy?" Awsten asked, a little anxiously.

"He is less strict than you were, but I was your boy first, and I shall be your servant always. You are going to get well and come back to us." My longing was so great that for a moment I believed my own words.

As if to contradict me, the coughing began, and I had to watch him helplessly. If only this agony might end, but though he had been dancer to the Muses, Dame Fortune would not let him die. The room seemed to get narrower, the air worse. I bent over him to catch what he was trying to say. "And who will look after my little Maudlyne now…," and I did not know if he were thinking of his daughter, or his love. Then Mistress Doggett thundered through the door, "That boy must go; he has been here an hour, and you have started your cough again with too much speech."

"I will not say another word, if you will let me stay."

"Thou must go, Sands," Awsten opened his eyes again, "the notary is expected, and before I speak with him I must rest. Ask Master Sly from me to let thee come next week."

I kissed his hand and knelt, trying to think of some word to comfort him, for we both knew that this was the last time we should be together. "If I could take your ills on me, Master Awsten," I stammered, because my grief was as sharp as his fever. "Courage," he whispered, "they will soon forget me, they never remember even kings." Then the head that had held a thousand of us silent lolled sideways on the pillow, and he dropped my hand. Mistress Doggett seized me by the belt, and forced me towards the door. "Master Awsten," I wailed in a dry, desperate whisper, and somehow he managed to look up. "Thou shalt have my lute, Sands, since thou hast liked my songs, the ones I sang to Maudlyne when I kissed her under the roses," and in the midst of all this misery, he smiled at Mistress Doggett, and then winked.

"Bless the gentleman, jesting and so ill," she began to laugh, and then the laughter turned to sobs.

"Dost think thou canst have thy way with me, just because I am abed?" Awsten joked with a flash of the old humour. He raised his hand in the same light gesture of farewell that it had been his custom to use on our sun-filled stage, when the flags, the galleries, and the heavy but momentarily hushed citizens had become his phantoms, and all that was solid was the sky. Then he dropped wearily back upon his pillows. "The notary! Why does he tarry so? Mistress Doggett, I pray you, send a messenger to speed him." Then he added, and we did not know if the words came from memory or fever, "Noon is past. Hurry. What is he waiting for? It is time for the prologue and the trumpets."

II

"Avoiding all playerly dashes."

THE GRAMMAR LECTURE.

Francis Beaumont.

Spring 1607.

HAT AILS THEE, SANDS?" Martin dangled his toes over the edge of the barge, so that they just did not touch the dirty water. "Wast beaten, to be so in the dumps?"

"First Master Awsten died, and now Master Sly has been sick these seven weeks." For an apprentice to lose his master was such a detriment to his fortunes that I wondered what would happen to me should the actor become worse.

"Enjoy thy freedom while thou hast it." Martin stretched himself, and hung his cap on a hook above us. "Oh, 'tis good to be alive on Sundays."

"We have paid dearly enough for our liberty today; that sermon this morning lasted two full hours."

"And are we any the better for listening to old Bentwood?" Martin swung the bit of rope that he was holding viciously round his head, as if he would have liked to hurl it at the preacher.

"God bless us, no! His words made me monstrous angry, they were so uncharitable."

Life was uncertain enough, without men denouncing harmless things as sinful. When Martin and I were together on what we called "our barge," we were too happy to bear grudges, or to envy the citizens their velvets and their horses; yet if some busybody found us here, especially after Bentwood's peroration, there would be the usual grumble at the idle prentice, and a stick about our shoulders. On Sundays we were supposed to be out shooting at the butts.

Martin began to twist his rope into a beautiful knot; provided that he had something in his hands, he was less restless than I was, and could sit still for hours. "Dost know what I heard Mother Crofton say, as I slipped out of the wash house?" he asked, as gaily as if he had won a new sixpence.

"Something foolish, no doubt."

"She was muttering to Kate, 'What can that sailor lad and the player's boy have in common? 'Tis an ill-assorted pair.'"

"And added, I suppose, that we should speedily end on the gallows."

"Not this noon. That will come tonight when she counts her marchpane pies," and Martin pulled a suspiciously bulky cloth out of his wallet.

"We shall be beaten."

"But the pies will be in our bellies. Courage, Sands, there are but two of them. She is weak at ciphering, and may not notice."

I stretched out my hand; it was perfection added to the day. "Fate is strange," I said. "If thine uncle had not sold his house..."

"And I had not been his ward ..."

"Thou hadst never come to lodge with us this winter." We chanted the last sentence together, as if we were pages in an interlude. It was our private language, separating us from the rest of the household, and making us brothers.

"The first time that I saw thee, Sands" (he would never call me James, he said it was too regal a name), "I took thee for a Dutchman's monkey."

"Even Kate was scared to come within reach of thy great paws."

"But when it came to supper time, and I saw thee with thy trencher, I said, 'With an appetite like that, he's a Christian like the rest of us'!"

I was ashamed to confess to Martin how vehemently I

had prayed that first evening that he would leave. His uncle was the navigator of the *Seagull,* and had already taken his nephew with him on a voyage. Martin had seemed so raw, so big, that although he was hardly six months older than I was, I had thought of him as a man. For over a week I had sat apprehensively opposite him at table, until one noon Master Sly had sent me upon some errand, and by the time that I had returned, the company had dined and the board was cleared. Before I could go into the kitchen, a heavy fist had fallen on my shoulder. I had looked up, expecting Martin to twist my arm "to make the jackanapes dance," as some of the youths did if they caught me. To my surprise, he had thrust a pot of meat into my hands. "Timothy knocked two newly washed sheets off the line," he had whispered gruffly. "Save me, Sands, if our mate has not fewer oaths in his tarry mouth than Mother Crofton! 'Twas the world's wonder! Mark you, we dared not laugh. So I kept this for thee, but go eat it in the yard. I had rather my uncle caught me sleeping on the yard-arm than front that sauce-box before evening." From that moment, as Sly complained, we had played and chattered together "like a tumble of bear cubs." There was a loyalty under Martin's rough ways that my better-schooled companions lacked. And what tales he could tell me! I was never tired of hearing about his adventures; they made me forget my master's uncertain temper and the draughty chinks in our attic.

It was early in March, but although the sun was out the air was still asleep. There were only a few wherries crossing the Thames. Our elders preferred the fireside, but I pulled my cloak round me again, drew my knees up under its folds, and ventured, "How big are the Indies when you get to them?" I had learned that if I pressed Martin to speak about his voyage, he was confused and soon silent, but that if I asked him a question he would answer it, and then the reply would remind him of something else, until we ended, off any known map, in some mariner's imagination.

"Some of the islands rise out of the sea like a bush on waste ground, others are as big as a county."

"Doesn't it feel like trespassing to sail among them? How can your captain find his way?"

"By the sun and the stars. It is a difficult art, but my uncle is teaching it to me. He says that once you have learnt it, it is easier than to take a short cut from London Bridge to Paul's."

"I should be afraid of all the monsters you have told me about, the fish with the red, snapping gills, and those sharks."

Martin shrugged his shoulders. "Look you, Sands, if the wind blows you overboard in the Narrows, you will die from the cold, and if your fingers slip from a rope because the sun has blistered them, the sharks will eat you; it comes to the same thing in the end."

I looked up at him admiringly, because I doubted whether

I should have the courage to climb a mast, even in harbour, and he had been out on the yards, in a gale. "But are the islands worth such perils once you reach them?" I asked.

"At first I was afraid of the green. There are leaves everywhere, trees taller than ships, strange shrubs, and no clearings. Even at anchor, we had the feeling that creepers might twine themselves along our ropes while we were asleep. One man said that he felt they would strangle him. And what I cannot describe to you is the heat. You Londoners grumble when Lambeth marsh stinks on a thundery day, and the houses are full of flies. But in the Indies the air is soft, and the body of the heat gets into you, until you lie on planks like frying pans, and groan for a breeze. Nor is it cooler at night. It is only as the light comes that there is sometimes a little wind. Then I used to climb to the mast head and look down at the flying fish, trimble-tremble between the waves, or watch the dawn rising above the palms, the colour of a dry biscuit."

"Oh," I said, but thinking of our icy, hungry winters, this did not seem so terrible, "it would be easier to endure the heat than gales."

"It is partly the frieze we wear. I wanted to take off my shirt, but the captain forbade it. He was wrong, the natives suffered less than we did from chills."

"Yet thine uncle said the other evening that the savages had bows and arrows; wast not afraid to go ashore?"

"Only where the Spaniards have beaten them and taught them to hate us. We paid our islanders for what we needed, and at our anchorage they showed us where the best water was, and brought us fish; and when they dumped a net full on the deck, they were such colours and shapes that we might have been looking at one of their sunsets." Martin hauled some shells out of a little bag that he carried at his belt. I had seen them before, but was never tired of looking at them; one was almost an ivory beetle, and another was a frosted branch that my companion said was coral. "The fish are somewhat flat in savour, I think it is the warmth of the seas, we all preferred our English herrings."

"Did the women come aboard as well? It must be strange to see them without farthingales, simply in aprons."

"They are as nature made them," Martin answered shortly, "and not like our Southwark maids, always wondering how much a man has in his wallet. But we saw them only ashore. Women on a ship bring quarrels."

"But how could you speak to the natives? Did one of the crew know their language?"

"Words are not so necessary as you players think." Martin slapped me playfully on the shoulder and laughed. "There is always barter. I remember I was scaling an anchor chain one morning, when I saw a canoe with three natives in it coming towards the ship. There they were, bobbing up and down in the surf till it almost made me sea-sick to look at them. The middle fellow had some sort of board, they seem not to row as we do, and the man next to him, I suppose he was the chief, had nothing on except a clout and an alderman's hat! I stared, and then I saw a pelican flying behind them in the identical bumpy way that the paddles dipped. Flip, flop, flip, flop, there was something so droll about it that I burst out laughing. They came alongside and offered us a great basket of some nuts that grow there, hairy, great husks filled with the coolest drink you ever tasted. And when we looked over the side to offer them some rags of silk in exchange, we found that the chief was wearing my uncle's hat, an old beaver that had hung in his cabin throughout the voyage, with salt all over the crown, and a bare patch where it had rubbed against the wall. One of our crew must have traded it for a trifle on the previous day, though we could never find the culprit."

"What did thine uncle do?"

"Oh, he laughed. The chief thought there was magic in it, something to do with the winds, and then it was uncommon good fortune that we could not talk to him."

"Yet once thou hadst seen those wonders, wast thou not glad to come home?"

"There is no sight more beautiful than Plymouth harbour rising from the sea on a cool September morning, and nothing fairer than to glide in, knowing that pirates and perils are behind you. Yes, I was glad enough to stretch my legs and eat my fill for a week or two; but believe me, Sands, had it not been for thine antics and thy company, I should have fretted myself to a shadow during the winter. In the Indies there is room for all; we are free and equal, and a man is what he can make of himself. You Londoners cling so to degree. I have to doff my cap to some old justice who would stop a morris because of his own weak legs, and nothing is to be changed, because this is grandfather's custom and the old man has to be cosseted. Remember Dr Bentwood! He had Lucy thrust out of the borough because she slept with a lad behind the bushes, but the cross-tempered scold who denounced her is to go straight to heaven! She has never missed one of his dismal sermons. No, in the islands if a man's knife snaps on a root, the jungle will cover him almost before his comrades have missed him; but if he has luck, and is not scornful of the native hunters, there are no boundaries, he is his own master."

"Even so, thou wilt not sail again this summer, wilt thou? I should miss thee terribly."

"Why, Sands, we are due at Greenwich in another week, to begin loading the stores."

"Oh, Martin, no! I have been saving pennies so that we could go to the great morris on May Day."

Martin looked at me patiently, as if my landlubber's ignorance were inexplicable. "But by May, Sands, if we are to bring our cargo home without wintering abroad, we must be well past the Azores."

"Oh," I moaned, "I hoped we should have had the summer together." The water smelt rancid that had seemed so silvery, and there was an ugly splinter that I had never noticed before, sticking crookedly out of the rail. My companion put his rope down on the deck and scratched his ear, as if he were trying to find some way to comfort me. "Look," he said slowly, "every craft has its mystery, and I laughed till I choked at Christmas when thou wast the little page with the great wooden sword, rattling after the Fool. Thou hast mastered thy trade as I try to master mine, but does it really make thee happy to stand up in a ruff and stomacher, and squeak of thy virtue as if thou wast a maid with the green sickness?"

I shook my head.

"I thought as much. Thou art no more fitted to thy task than I should be to an inkpot if they had bound me to a scrivener. Look thee, Sands, after the *Seagull* has been loaded they will give us leave for a day, and thou must make shift to get to Greenwich. I'll contrive a place for thee in the hold, and there thou must hide till we are well out in the Narrows. The captain may give thee a clout or two at first, but he will be glad of an extra pair of hands, and by the time we return, thou wilt be a man, and we will make our voyages together, and never be separated."

"Be a sailor!" I said stupidly.

"Why not? 'Tis a hard life, but show me one better."

"Alas, I have not thy muscles."

"Nor, a spring ago, had I! Thou wilt harden thy shoulders hauling ropes, and toughen thy belly chewing thongs, but take thy fill of Mother Crofton's suppers, we shall make merry on bilge water and weevils once we are a day out from land."

"But they will seize me as a runaway when we return."

"Not with thy skin tanned to leather, and a seaman's paws. Besides," Martin was almost trembling with excitement, "if thou likest the islands, must we ever come home?"

"Look what I have to leave," I said.

"Leave, Sands?" Martin stared at me in astonishment, and as I gazed down at the grey scum, the dead dog, and the dirty, tattered caps floating slowly past with the tide, I nodded. "Thou art right, there is nothing."

"It is only the journey to Greenwich that will be difficult."

"Hast thou forgotten? Mother Crofton has a sister married to a journeyman there, and is always sending her parcels by the carrier. If I wash her kitchen floor for a while, she might beg leave for me to take one of the bundles instead. I can plead that I want to say farewell to thee."

"And I'll paint that bucket tomorrow, the one that she has been after me to mend, all winter."

"Oh, Martin, I fear I shall disgrace thee, I shall never climb that mast."

"Go to, thou wilt, with me." Martin jumped to his feet, grinning wickedly. "Come quickly, I see the prentices return- ing with their bows, and my uncle will be suspicious if we are late." He stepped lightly on to the rail, and swarmed up the mooring rope as if it had been a ladder. "Come, Sands," he mocked, leaning over to watch me, with his hands on his knees, while I scrambled up the easier way, digging my toes and fingers into the crevices of some old, now broken steps. "Thou hast aped a maid so long that it is time I taught thee to stand on thine own two legs. So... so... give me thy hand," and, shouting with laughter, he hauled me up the last great stone, to stand beside him on the wharf.

The catkins danced above the neighbouring hedge. One of the country girls had brought some windflowers back from a Sunday walk, but they did not like captivity, they were fading. "It's spring," people said, if I came to them upon an errand; but although I was thankful that the winter was over, April was a harsh season. It was not a time of love and gentleness as they pretended, but the moment when the heart longed for change so intensely that it seemed to detach itself from the body in an agony of wishing. Everything could happen, and nothing did. I had had no news from Martin, and unless his plan succeeded, the days would go by and midsummer come, with my horizon (that could have been an empire) bounded by our street.

All the weeks were the same. There was a crack in the stool where somebody had kicked it years before, I could tell the time, not by the sun dial, but by sounds and voices, "Where hast thou put my broom, girl?" followed by Mother Crofton's footsteps in the yard; "Cress, fresh water cress," and you knew that the stuff had been plucked yesterday and was already wilting, ending, a little before noon, with the hooves of the carrier's horse, ringing on the cobbles. It was Lent; we had no rehearsals, but we should soon be shouting some wild lord's adventures in the spring play, and the populace would follow us without a groan, or as much as an orange pip, because it was the moment when all had a will to go wandering. Yet the words would be only words, the wishes, wishes. Martin had sent no message, and the certain things in life were Bentwood's texts or my master's grumbles.

"Boy."

"Here, sir."

"Go to the *Plough,* and fetch me a jug of ale. Oh, this gout! It rips the courage out of a man, 'tis worse today than it was on Sunday."

Mr Sly was leaning against the back of the settle, with his leg stretched out on a stool in front of him. He had been ailing and irritable ever since he had had an ague the previous autumn, and nothing that we did was right for him. "'Tis all that sack he drinks," Mother Crofton had repeated, until he had caught her a great, whacking blow on her behind, and commanded her to hold her peace. Now she would only look first at the beaker, then at us, and wink, so that Mr Sly, if he happened not to see this, wondered why we laughed. Yet she loved him more than she had loved my first master, Awsten. Sly was warmer, nearer to her; he never brought her a knot of ribbon nor a half-worn coat, as Awsten had sometimes done, but he drank to her. She was always his first toast, as if she had been his lady.

I held my hand out for the money to pay for the ale, and Mr Sly looked up sharply. "Mind, boy, no loitering, I'm expecting thy playfellow's uncle to visit me, and if thou art nimble in fetching us our drink, mayhap he will give thee news of thy comrade."

"Martin's uncle! I thought he was at Greenwich."

"And so he was, but we have business together. Now, boy, hurry." He reached for his stick, but before he could clout me, I was running down the road.

How different the morning looked now! On most occasions I should have loitered, and risked a beating. Today, a pony could hardly have been swifter. Martin would send me a message, but I could not expect his uncle to look for me. Perhaps the voyage had been abandoned altogether? In another year I should be older and stronger; besides, there was a place that I had never shown him, where the swans nested on the other side of Southwark marsh. The spot in winter was knee-deep in mud. Oh, Martin, I thought, Martin, come back to me.

The weeks since he had left had been a nightmare of loneliness. Everything had gone wrong; I had had a cold myself, and one of those irritating, lingering coughs that woke me at night and choked me at table. It had been cold one day and hot the next, and now the plague deaths were increasing. "It's the Scots," all London grumbled, "they have brought the rains with them, as well as their fleas. Nothing has been the same since Queen Elizabeth died."

I was out of breath by the time that I got as far as Widow Skinner's house. She hated players, and I crossed to the far side of the road. It would not be the first time that she had emptied her slops from a top window as one or other of us passed. A merchant trotted by on a tall roan horse. I dodged a serving maid, jumped over a hole, and ran, panting, into the *Plough*.

"My floor!" the innkeeper's wife groaned, leaning on her broom. "Be careful, boy, 'tis newly sanded."

"But it's dry outside." I waited anxiously at the threshold, hoping that she would not notice the trail of dust.

"And how is thy master, Sands?" Mr Humphries, the innkeeper, asked kindly. "When I saw him last on Sunday he was of an evil, liverish colour."

"He has the gout, but he says it is the weather."

"His health will improve when Lent is over. This is no season for Mr Sly, nor for me either." Humphries was a portly fellow who had been a quarterstaff champion in his youth, and could demolish a capon and a quarter joint of lamb easily at a sitting.

"'Tis good that thou hast to fast once a year," his wife called from the kitchen. "Here, child, I must not break the church rules by giving thee a cake," she continued, as she came back with a trencher, "but this manchet is fresh from a loaf that I baked only yesterday, and there's country butter on it." She was fond of boys and had none of her own.

"Of a verity, my master is ill-pleased when he is not playing," I said. "As soon as the flag goes up, he forgets that he is ailing."

"And he is right, boy, he is right. No honest man enjoys being idle; remember this when thy comrades tempt thee to dawdle. It's your lack-a-purpose fellows that sour the world; they drink water, and it leads them to sermons. If they chopped wood, or heaved barrels round for their living, like the rest of us do, they would drink their ale, sleep like babes, and leave words to lawyers' clerks."

I nodded without answering, because I was impatient to return home, but Master Humphries continued, "Oh, I know you gentlemen players laugh, but believe me, it is a serious matter. These Puritans will infect the city. Unless the citizens join together and suppress them soon, they will close the theatres before thy beard has grown, and then it will be the turn of the alehouses and taverns."

The Puritans had less a poor imagination than too much of

it. They insisted that acting was a form of falsehood, because no man should pretend to be other than he was. Yet they found slanders, where we heard only the rustling of summer leaves; and if they hated the Court, it was less because of its wickedness than because a courtier's monopoly interfered with their trade. "Search their zeal," I had heard a clown say once, still secure in the protection of his coat, "they have a godly exterior, but what is in their hearts? Gold, my masters, not prayers."

I took up the jug, but the innkeeper lifted his hand. "Not so swift, boy, wait, I have a present for thy master." So there I had to stand, shuffling from one foot to the other, while we listened to Humphries' shoes clattering down the cellar steps, and I swallowed my bread and butter in such gulps that I hardly tasted it.

"Thou hast spring in thy legs," his wife said, rubbing at a spot on the table. "I was the same when I was young. Now the maypoles will be here, and April over, before I have had time to clean the house."

"It's Martin," I answered, "rather than the season. His uncle is coming up from Greenwich today and, if I am back in time, may give me news of him."

"He's a rough lad to be thy playfellow, but they say that contrasts bring out the colour of a cloak, and if so, why should it not be the same for human beings? Mayhap it is thy gentleness; 'tis good thou art a player's boy, no other craft would have fitted thee half as well."

"I can hold my own in a bout of fence," I said indignantly, and the goodwife smiled.

"The sword's a gentleman's weapon. Prentices use staves." She smiled at me, as if she could read my secret thoughts, the ones I had not confessed even to Martin.

If I had been a girl, I should have blushed. Perhaps it was Master Awsten's example, but I wanted to be a page. Not for an hour in somebody's cast-off hose, but at a manor, in the country. The others would call it pride, but I was willing to be as humble as a child. It was only that I wanted to escape from the rough words and the dirt, and from the never distant terror of the plague.

"Thou art grown enough for thy years," Mistress Humphries continued, "but next summer thy companion, Martin, will be a man. Then he will look for a maid, and thou wilt be neither babe nor full-fledged hawk. We must find thee a companion of thine own age."

"I am almost as old as Martin," I protested.

"But there is a world of difference between you. Martin is a good lad, and devoted to his uncle, but four walls will never hold him; while with thee, child," she looked at me kindly, "I know not what I should say. Thou hast brawn," she poked me playfully in the doublet that was becoming too tight for me, "but thou lackest something...hast thou been born under the Moon?"

"The Moon! Who talks of the Moon?" Humphries came

back into the kitchen, with a bottle held carefully under his arm. "Tell Mr Sly to drink Rhenish at the crescent, Burgundy when it is at the full, and sack at all times. Then I shall not mope as I do now for want of his merry stories. And now, young Sands, carry this back to him, as if it were an egg that might slip out of thy clumsy fingers. 'Tis the best I have in my cellar, and is meant to oil his joints so that he can soon come and pass an evening with me."

I saw a familiar figure as I came towards our door, but I dared not run for fear of spilling the ale or dropping the wine. "Please, sir," I panted, as we met at the threshold, "how is Martin?"

"Martin! Where are thy manners, child? Never a good morrow, but how is that foolish nephew of mine? I have not come all the way from Greenwich to give thee news about thy playmate." Then he relented and added, "He is not in favour with me at present; the boy has grown so tall that I have had to buy him two new suits of clothes. But he sent thee his greetings; and now, lead me in to thy master."

Mother Crofton was already waiting at the door to welcome him, and take his cloak. "Give you good morrow, sir," Sly's great voice boomed from the chimney seat, "the gout is my jailor; and till my bill of delivery is come, I cannot rise to greet you, as I would wish."

"I am much grieved, good sir, to find you so afflicted. I

had rather face a three day gale myself than be tortured by these joint pains, particularly if they be combined, as they often are, with an ague."

I went forward, bowed, and put the wine on the table. "Master Humphries was much affected to hear of your illness, and sent you this from his cellar."

"Humphries is a good friend." Sly picked up the bottle. "Nay, we have glasses, do not wait to pour it. Be off with you for an hour, there is wood to stack in the yard, we have business to discuss and shall not require thee."

I bowed again and went into the passage, but was careful not to close the door completely. Mother Crofton had hung a curtain up to keep the draught from Master Sly's leg, and I hid myself in a fold of it. I wanted to know if the *Seagull* was going to sail; besides, unless I was present when the navigator left, how could I ask if Martin had sent me some other message?

When I peeped through the crack of the door a few moments later, Martin's uncle was sitting upright on a stool. In his plain doublet he looked like a country gentleman. He put some papers down on the table in front of him, and asked in so low a voice that I could hardly hear the question, "Have you thought any further about my proposition, Mr Sly?"

Sly shifted his leg on the cushion; he seemed to be a little uneasy. "I have spoken to some of my friends about you, but the fellows who have the will to venture have no ryals, and those with a crown or two to spare are unwilling to risk them now on voyages. The King has no care for the fleet."

"Yes, times have changed. When the Queen was alive, even the corsairs were afraid of us; now if we sail into a foreign port, the dirtiest harbour urchins spit and laugh. But what can we expect?" He banged the table in his anger. "The Spaniards know well enough that the King will not lift a finger to protect the ships that are, after all, a part of his realm. I could weep with the shame of it."

"There is much to be said for staying quietly at home."

"Yet you want your spices and your wine. And what would you do with your wool, if you could not sell it abroad?"

"I agree, good sir, I agree, but I bless Fortune that she has not called me to be a merchant."

"And then the King claps the wisest captain that we ever had into the Tower, and I cannot cross London Bridge for feathers. The fools stuff them in their hats as if they were reeds around a trap, and the way they sniff nosegays reminds me of chamberwomen."

"Men say that Ralegh plotted against the King."

"With the Spaniards? With his life-long enemies? It is making asses of the citizens to ask us to believe it."

"All the same, the Londoners did not like him; they said he was too proud."

"Because he had a mind that winged above their petty rivalries. He soared too high and too far."

"They said he was an atheist."

"The sparrows! If a man lifts himself a quill's length above his fellows, they call him atheist and rogue. No, Sir Walter knew the answer to our problems. We have more people and less money every year. Sail to the West, he said, sail to the West...."

"And be eaten by men with eyes at the back of their shoulders. No, I would rather put up with my troubles at home."

"This will be my fourth voyage to the Indies. Granted a good ship, it is less perilous, believe me, sir, than to walk at Moorgate on a holiday among brawlers with unbaited swords."

"I have known half a dozen fellows put to sea to seek their fortunes. Only one of them returned, with a shirt less than when he went away."

"But there is land. Last summer a native took me up a hill, and to right and left of us I saw little but spice bushes. Further away, on the mainland, he said there was gold. Anyhow, I had no beggars whining at my heels."

"And no good wine." Master Sly lifted his glass, and they drank to one another. "No, sir, London with all its faults is good enough for me."

"I was not suggesting, Master Sly, that anyone of your capacity should settle in the Indies. No, all I need is to find some gentleman willing to take the eighth of a share in our venture. If I give another bond to those grasping Greenwich chandlers, we shall lose the profit of any cargo we may land, before we have set our sails."

He has Martin's eyes, I thought, as I peeped cautiously round the edge of the door, and like his nephew he was quiet and determined. The discussion was not new to me; it had been going on all winter. "My uncle was one of Ralegh's men," Martin had whispered during the first evening, and the navigator was full of the same vision as his master, and like all mariners, contemptuous of the new policies of the King. "Let him make peace with Spain, if he will," he had grumbled continuously, "but if it had not been for the ships, he would have had neither realm nor riches to inherit."

Sly began to crumble a pellet of bread between his fingers. "The only man I could interest," he said, "is a fellow I mistrust... young Moryson."

"He is penniless, I suppose."

"Strangely enough, no. He is a studious fellow with the pate of an owl, and without a single Christian pursuit. He spends his days poring over ciphers. Think of it! He says that if we knew more about the winds, it might be possible to foretell what the weather would be next Sunday!"

"Moryson! The heir to Sir Nicholas Jenkinson? I think I have heard the name."

"When I spoke to him concerning your venture, what do you think he said! 'I've no mind to his gold, but if he

is a navigator, could he collect some observations for me?'
'Not interested in gold!'" Sly sat up so angrily that his toe
touched the table leg, and he groaned. "He's another of
your master's persuasion, if you ask me, only interested in
subjects in which it is not meet for us to dabble."

"Gold! 'Tis a strange substance. We can die for lack of it;
yet mark you, if a beggar and I have a fever, will lying on a
bed of it make any difference to our sufferings?"

"Prithee, good my master, speak for yourself. Five rose
nobles in my palm this moment would go far to allay the
gout. I should hop, if need be, to Goodman Wilson's shop,
and order a cloak of his best velvet; yes, and have it lined
with peach-coloured satin. By the time that he had fitted
it, my legs would be as nimble as those of a jigging fool
in May."

"No." Martin's uncle shook his head. "There are discov-
eries to be made that would be worth more to us than ryals.
The Indians gave a cordial to Sir Walter that quells a fever
within the space of a day. And beyond the great river that I
saw myself, they told us of a fountain whose waters can cure
the plague. Nay, if an old man take but a sip of them, he
rises like the phoenix, a youth of twenty once more."

"It would be an ill wind for the young heirs if their grand-
sires never died, though we should need fewer lawyers,"
Sly said, and they both laughed. "I sent word to Master
Moryson of your coming," Sly continued, "and he asks you

to wait upon him at his lodging, after you have dined with me. But remember my warning, and be careful. Collect nothing for him that you could not honestly declare to the parson, if he asked you of it."

"Oh, I know these students. They pretend to be indifferent to riches, and draw you up a contract tighter than any dealer in spices could devise. Besides, they are usually men ambitious to step above their degree."

"It is the fashion of the day. Nobody is content with his calling any longer. I caught my own apprentice leading a knight's horse from the *Plough* to the blacksmith, just because he would rather follow a satin sleeve than his own craft."

"He caught that from his first master, Gentleman Phillips. 'Tis a strange lad, but my nephew likes him, and that reminds me, Martin wants to show his playfellow the *Seagull*. Would you give Sands leave to return with me tomorrow, and I would send him back to you on Thursday, in the care of a pilot who is a good friend of mine."

I almost burst out of my hiding place to throw myself at my master's feet, and beg for the holiday, but Mother Crofton pushed me behind her and bustled first into the room. She had a platter of meat in her hands. "Let the boy go," she entreated, "then he can take a parcel to my sister. Patience and I were brought up as if we were twins, and since she married that great Timothy of hers, when have I seen her? Once since the marriage, and that was two years ago come Michaelmas." She dabbed her eyes with the corner of her apron.

"Sands is sluggish enough without going on a holiday," Sly complained, but without much conviction.

"It's Lent, no theatres are open, let the little wag have the three days, not for his sake, but for my Martin."

"It is hard to refuse you a boon when you are about to leave our Christian world for your archipelago of monsters. Besides, I shall miss you, good friend, your stories have given me what I cannot get from the playhouse because I am of it, and that is entertainment throughout our winter evenings. Take him then, but remember, if he is impudent, a rope's end will benefit the rascal amazingly. Hast been listening?" he asked fiercely, for he saw me standing behind Mother Crofton's shoulder. But she answered for me, "Nay, the lad has been stacking wood. I called him in myself a moment since, to help me set the table."

Martin had left me sitting in the shipyard, on a barrel that was almost hidden behind a heap of planks and rusty bolts. He had gone to the *Seagull* to make sure that only the watchman was on deck, then we were going to slip together into the hold. On this last night the crew were ashore, and as Martin had assured me, "Old Sam wouldn't wake if a rat ran over his head." The rim of the cask cut into my legs, and the air was so heavy with dried fish and stale water that I drew my cloak over my mouth to keep out the poisonous vapours. Perhaps it was the smell that made me queasy; the events of the day turned round and round in my head, until I longed for my old pallet in Southwark and a good night's sleep.

Our plans had gone smoothly, too smoothly, I thought; nobody had doubted us. Martin's uncle had found a friend on the boat, and I had been able to sit alone at the bow, and watch the banks as we had drifted rather than sailed down the Thames. Martin had been working with the riggers, when we had arrived at the *Silver Dolphin* where his uncle lodged, so that I had had time to take Mother Crofton's parcel to her sister, who lived only a couple of streets away. They had made much of me there, and would have had me stay to dinner, but after I had explained that I had been given the holiday to say farewell to my friend, they had thrust a pie into my hands and sent me back to the inn. I had seen Martin directly I had turned the corner, he was standing in a great frieze jerkin with leather patches at the elbows, looking eagerly up the road. We had shouted greetings; I had run forward, and was the first to clap him on the shoulder, but then as we had stood in front of one another, I knew that he had changed.

He had grown even taller during the month since I had seen him, his speech was thick with new oaths, and I had felt, as he gazed at me, that he was, in some way, disappointed. "God bless me, why hast thou come in thy stage doublet?" he had asked. "Dost think the salt will treat thee with more respect?" I had hung my head, because it was the thickest garment that I possessed, and had muttered, "I have no other."

The afternoon had dragged, our easy comradeship was over, there was some barrier between us. He had even mocked me about my trade. "Thou must unlearn that player's English, or my shipmates will laugh at thee." Then he had felt my muscles in dismay, and had moaned, shaking his head, "Mind thou dost not curtsey to the mate, when we turn out to reef the sails." This was not the dream that had drawn me to Greenwich. I wanted to go to some new island and depend upon myself in the adventure. I longed to be Martin's comrade, but I also wanted to remain James Sands, with all his fantasies and hopes, not to turn into some wrinkled sea dog, with an empty head, a careless tongue, and a belly clamouring for beer.

The wind blew round my knees. I was trembling with cold, and the air had changed my collar into a damp and dirty rag. I saw myself hauled on deck by some iron-fisted sailor, and kicked towards the captain. How could I ever climb those ropes? Everywhere was sinister in this dusk. I looked up and almost screamed. A man in a hood was coming towards me in the dark. Perhaps he had mistaken me for a thief? Then the shape turned into a fragment of canvas flapping from a pole. I shivered, I was lonely, I longed for Mother Crofton's familiar kitchen and the logs blazing on the hearth. Perhaps this was all a mistake and it was better to admit it now, while there was still time to mend it. But the Indies, the scarlet-feathered birds, the bursting apricot sun above the spice bushes, the delicate shells.... I rocked up and down, torn between longing and fear.

I heard a step in the yard. This time it really was Martin. He came towards me with a thick cloak that he had begged or borrowed over his arm. A silver ring dangled from each of his ears. I knew, as I looked up, that under the surface our friendship was as deep as ever; he wanted me as much as I needed him; with will and effort I could make myself into a sailor. "Fix thy mind on thy desire, boy," Master Awsten had often said to me, "and in time thou wilt achieve it." I jumped from the cask, and felt a nail rip my sleeve. "Look what I have found," Martin said gaily, holding out the cloak, "even a nor-wester can't penetrate this!" Then I felt sea-sick although I was standing on firm ground. I remembered the choking water when, before I had been breeched, I saw a heaving mass of sea, and myself, ignorant and frightened, sliding from the slippery ropes as the *Seagull* pitched. "I cannot come," I moaned. "I want to go with thee, but I can't; oh, Martin, I should only disgrace thee, thou wilt have to leave me. I cannot climb those yards...forgive me, Martin, but I should only slide overboard. I suppose I belong ashore."

III

Bellario.

HE SUN WAS UP. I had discovered a fallen tree that was almost as comfortable as a settle, and Master Sly had given me my freedom until evening. Everything was growing again; under the marsh-lily leaves the water was not unbearably cold, and scratching away the dry, rusty leaves at my feet, I saw a patch of violets. The glade might have been the arbour of a manor house, because the windflowers swept from bush to bush in diamonds and squares, and just below my perch, instead of a sun dial on the grass, there were two small daffodils. I had never seen them wild in a wood before, only in gardens.

"Why, boy, thou hast discovered my favourite pool. I thought the river-god hid it from the eyes of mortals. Art a changeling?" I had heard no footsteps on the moss, and I jumped. A tall man in a wonderfully fair ash-coloured suit, slashed with murray, stepped in front of me. He held a rough stick in his hand, and was apparently as astonished as I was myself.

"I crave your pardon, good sir, I did not know that I was trespassing."

"Sit still, sit still." He motioned me to stay where I was. "There is room for both of us on that tree. What art thou binding together with thy long grasses?"

"'Tis a wreath for my late master; he also called me a changeling."

"Thy late master! I have just spoken to Mr Sly. He was sitting on a bench outside the *Green Dragon,* drinking ale, and very vividly alive. I know thou must be his boy, because I saw thee yesterday with the horses."

"Then you are Mr Beaumont!" I sprang up and made my reverence. "Believe me, sir, I have disturbed no beast, and these few flowers come from the hedges I passed, as I walked here."

"I like a youth to be at home in the woods," the deep voice growled. "Sit down again, and tell me about thy garland; art trying to recover thy lost childhood?"

I shook my head. "I should not want to be a child again, it would be as dissembling as play-acting."

"And thou a player's boy!" Mr Beaumont laughed until the tears came into his eyes. "Wert pressed to thy calling against thy will?"

"No, Master Phillips chose me, but he is dead. It is hard to follow another master."

"Go to, dost still remember him? The young are seldom loyal."

"Master Awsten came to me in our orchard like a god. He died, but that was later, like an emperor."

"Yes, Phillips could act. I remember seeing him when I was a young man, and shows still meant something to me."

"And do they mean nothing to you now, sir?" I forgot in my astonishment to be timid.

"I have too many in my own head. Life or the Tilt Yard or this very hour, all is semblance, all fantasy. Why, if we knew the right word, boy, like Pythagoras, we could dissolve these shadows."

"And fly?" It was my turn to smile.

"Perhaps, or be nothing, feel nothing, never want a cloak in December, nor spring water in July."

"I should like there to be no more winter," I replied, "but it would be wonderful strange never to rake the hay, nor hear the doves."

"Would it? I could give up everything, I think, to be free from these fevers," he passed his hand across his forehead, "except these daffodils. All our innocence is in them."

"I should mind giving up the memory of Master Awsten."

"Then I see that thou art a lover," and he smiled.

"I am uncertain that I know what love is," I answered cautiously, "the poets describe it as madness."

"Dost suppose they are right? Our host of the *Dragon* would say that it was an excellent occasion to draw more ale."

"But the poets come like a sun into our thoughts. They light them up, so that we may understand them."

"May be. Or dost thou wait, perhaps, to have a popinjay drop into thy lap, without thy serving time for it?"

I looked up in such amazement that he began to laugh again. "Poor child, do not listen to a greybeard like myself. Finish thy garland, and sing me a song."

"You are no greybeard, you are like what my master was, a king." He had flung his hat on to the ground beside him, and there was not a white hair in his head. Everything was young about him except his eyes; there was such a deep melancholy in these when I looked up that I was almost afraid.

"Flatterer!" Mr Beaumont tapped me lightly on the shoulder. "I warn thee, boy, truth is the Gorgon's head, if thou hast ever heard that tale. It petrifies those who look upon it, and they die, at least to their fellow men."

"Tell me the story," I begged.

"Study the philosophers, child, if thy real desire is to have learning."

"No," I shook my head resolutely. "What does it matter to me what the Romans did, furlongs from here? We had our Golden Age, we had Arthur," and I began to sing.

"In Camelot, in Camelot,
on a bitter day,
they drove the lovely maid,
Mercy, away;
she left us the dotted thorn
and a knot of may."

I could see that Mr Beaumont misliked my words, but it was what I felt.

"Thou canst not know the world till thou hast read the Latins," he scolded; then he added, "I forgive thee thy ballads, boy, thou art young, and April wakes the blood."

"I do not want to be young. I would rather be of middle age, and have men listen, when I want to better what is wrong."

"'Twill come soon enough, what dost thou want to change?"

"Some of the ordinances that fetter us poor prentices."

"Child, child, thou fond and foolish babe! That is asking to grapple with the very order of the realm. Why, thou wilt tell me next it is thy ambition to write a tragedy!"

"Every boy in Southwark would have died for Master Awsten. He chose me for his service and taught me all I know, how to speak, salute," and I made the emperor's reverence to Mr Beaumont, "the way to draw and sheathe a sword. Then, as you have heard, good sir, he died. You cannot love twice."

"Oh, can't you!" Mr Beaumont looked amused.

"I am not thinking of maids," I said stiffly.

"Go to, thou art as serious as a preacher at St Gregory's. Is this to be a three hour sermon?"

"Very short, I need no liquorice for it."

"Well, thou shalt have my ear for as long as...that moor hen yonder is cleaning her feathers." He slid from the fallen tree to lie full length in the grass, but gently, so as not to disturb my heap of flowers. A fish splashed, the reeds rustled, and the daffodils in the patch of light seemed yellower than the sun.

"I spoke first of Master Awsten," I continued, "to show you that a prentice has no cares in a good home. It is the only time in his life that the younger son is treated as if he were his elder brother. But all masters are not like mine was. Some men take a boy simply to shake lice out of their jerkins, or to fetch them pots of ale. He is a servant whom they need not pay, and scarcely nourish. Then, later, if he bungles his craft because he has never learned it, out he goes to beg on the highways. I saw them hang a thief the other day, but the poor rogue had been taken from his mother's lap and taught to cut cloth short. Tell me, good sir, who was guilty? The knave, or his cheating master, the tailor? Then there are boys who find that they have been pressed into the wrong calling ..."

"Like thyself."

"I do not know," I said. "I like the ballads, but I am tired of being a virtuous maid in a white robe — I wish I could be a page."

"'Tis thy broad head. Thou art more mastiff than damsel, but in a year or two, inches will make thee an indifferent good gallant and, believe me, 'tis easier to play the gull than to write the foolishness he utters."

"If I had some speech worth saying ..."

"Then my Lord Citizen would hiss thee from the stage."

There was such indignation behind the words that I jumped, almost expecting a leather strap to whistle across my shoulders. Mr Beaumont had never forgiven the Londoners for bawling at his last comedy; though there were two sides to everything, as Master Sly had explained during our ride to Kent, and nobody liked to see his dignity turned inside out in front of his own servants, nor his wife's ambition gentled. All of them accepted Mr Beaumont as a scholar, but the theatre wasn't the Inner Temple, and it had cost the players thirteen shillings to repair the damages to their wardrobe. He, himself, had received a rotten orange, broadside on, in the middle of his new watchet-coloured slops, and the breeches had been ruined. If gentlemen wished to write plays, they might be as witty as they pleased; but not at the expense of their patrons, especially when these same patrons were ordinary folk, with an excellent appetite for beer, beef, and merriment, and not one line of Latin in their pates. No, he, Sly, had protested that the comedy was impossible.

If the rest of the company had listened to him — and he certainly had had more experience than most players, and if he might add this, the capacity to profit from it — what humiliations might have been avoided!

"We should change the world," I said, "why should the golden age be always behind us?"

"Because vision is not to be taught, boy, any more than your quarterstaff champion of the village green can be made into a master of fence."

"Yet unless there is reason in the universe, how can a prentice hope that his faithfulness will be rewarded?" I thought gloomily of the hours when I had been both the butt of Sly's discontent, and his nurse during his winter sickness.

"Or his sloth punished! Fie on thee, thou hast read too many broadsheets. Life is many things, but never the black and white of the first page of a primer."

"Then what is it?" I asked.

"Not even the philosophers can tell us, boy, but it is not the giving of comfits to the child who has read his lesson prettily. They say that the poet who brought us the Muses' names was murdered in Thessaly, and silver-voiced Wyatt was imprisoned in the Tower. Look at thine own hero, Arthur! No, we are not clipped patterns inside a cunningly contrived hedge; the years are a great sea, we cast our nets, and sometimes they are broken, and sometimes they bring us gold, for neither rhyme as I see it, nor reason."

I shook my head. I could not forgo Awsten's teaching. There was Virtue with a shining sword, on one side, and Vice, in his black and scarlet, on the other; so long as our deeds were piled in the right heaps, life was simple.

"What dost thou value, then," Mr Beaumont asked indifferently, "if not a girl or a venison pie?"

"Tenderness and loyalty as in this garland," and I held up my wreath.

His mood changed, and he pretended to examine the posy seriously. "I tell thee, boy, the next time that a play of mine finds favour with your orange spitters, I'll take thee as my page. Now what is this?" He pointed to the ragged robin. "Is it constancy?"

"Oh no, that is as ragged as the winds. To show we are steadfast, we use violets." Alas, the flowers that I handed to him were already beginning to fade.

"Faith, I should needs be a shepherd myself, to have time to learn these symbols! What hast thou for tranquillity if there be such a plant?" I lifted the fern that, dipped in water, kept my plunder fresh, and searched until I found a knot of stonecrop. This was not tall enough to catch the wind, and too lowly for a rosette, but Mr Beaumont shook his head. "It is the oleander root I want, boy, only it does not grow in Britain. The physician Theophrastus says it is a cure for melancholy. I would it could heal my wandering mind."

He looked in perfect health, in spite of his tale of fevers, but so dejected that I wondered what he had done to come into such conflict with the humours. Then his attention strayed, and I knew that he wanted to be alone. Oh, what a fool I had been! I had drawn the chance to meet one of the great wits of the age, only to weary him with my May-time antics. "Yes," I said, as I flung the garland into the stream, "we may stick flowers in our caps, but they will not bring us happiness." Then, because I knew that it was time for me to leave, I added in a burst of desperation, "I would I could be your page, and live for ever in your service."

"'Tis a sweet child," Mr Beaumont smiled, not with Awsten's gaiety, but gravely, as if from a distant and Thule-like land. "Come, I have a message for thy master, but thou shalt not take it to him hungry." He scrambled up from the ground, and with the movement the sadness seemed to drop away from him, and he added with a jester's mischief, "Has Mr Sly forgiven me yet for that pair of watchet slops? 'Twas a good deed, they were too liverish for his always ruddy complexion."

I had never been inside a manor before, and I had imagined it full of arras and great chairs, but the smallest chamber in a London merchant's house had richer furniture than this hall. The hangings were threadbare, and the chests battered with use. It did not belong to Mr Beaumont, but to his friend, a Kentish squire.

I hesitated at the door, but Mr Beaumont beckoned me to

follow him, with an impatient "Come in, boy, come in." We entered a study, looking over a rose garden, and a man got up from a settle, beside the fireplace. To my surprise, they both greeted each other as I might have shouted to a comrade, without ceremony or the compliments usual among gallants. "Forgive me, Mistress Ursula, I am late again. Your father is indulgent to my ways, but it is discourteous to keep the nymphs waiting."

I looked up, and saw a maid coming towards us, in a dress criss-crossed with tiny leaves, very lovely, but so unlike the city fashion, that when her spaniel bounded in front of her, I half expected the dog to turn into a unicorn.

"They are pestering me to write a comedy," Mr Beaumont continued, "but is it not a fault to sit in front of a blank sheet of paper on our first spring day!"

"Go to, Francis, you pen verses as easily as a throstle sings," the gentleman said. He had a kind voice, and he smiled at me.

"This is Sly's boy. I discovered him in the woods. The wag had found my favourite pool, and was sitting there on my own tree trunk! Grant me leave a moment longer, Mistress Ursula; I will but fetch a paper from your father's study, that I wish him to deliver to his master."

Both the gentlemen went out together, and I stood stupidly, with my cap in my hand, not knowing what to do.

"Art thou truly Mr Sly's apprentice?" Mistress Ursula

picked her spaniel up, and stared in astonishment at my rough doublet. "Is it not passing quiet here, after all the marvels of London?"

I shook my head. "The air in the woods is sweeter; besides, today is holiday."

"Oh, 'tis April, thou wouldst not like it in winter with the meadows sodden with snow. But if thou hast a day's liberty, dost thou not miss London the more, the brave sights, an ambassador to see perhaps, or an earl riding to Court with his attendants?"

"None of them are as beautiful as you are," I ventured; she was unlike any maid that I had seen, taller than I was, but about my age and without the affectations of the city misses, who alternately teased me or ignored me, if I were sent upon some errand to their fathers.

"Fie on thee for a pert knave! Come, leave dissembling and tell me about London. Mr Beaumont says, but I believe he mocks me, that there are Indians as red as cinnabar at the gardens."

"They are less red of skin than dark, more the sunburnt colour of a sailor. I saw them with my own eyes, and I was sorry for them, they were coughing in our damp mists."

"And hast thou been to the great fairs? Mr Beaumont has promised to take me to them after we are married, but this will not be for two full years." She sighed as innocently as any village maid, to whom the Moor in a morris is really a Sarazen and not the cobbler's son. We had heard about the betrothal in the village on the previous evening. "'Tis a strange match," the innkeeper had grunted, shaking his head, "neither of them has land, but Mr Beaumont and the Squire are like brothers."

"Perhaps the worthy gentleman your father will have occasion to visit London before that time?" I suggested.

"My father! Visit London! Nothing has got him from his books these twenty years." I could feel her mother speaking through Ursula's pretty indignation, the half scornful, half delighted voice of a woman who was proud of her husband's wit, but also resentful of his neglect of her. "Besides, Mr Beaumont honours us with his company so often, that my father says he has no need to ride up to the *Mermaid*; all the jests are brought back to him here, at his own table." She brushed a curl from her ear and smiled, as if I really were her playfellow. "Oh," I said, "I know what you would like best. There are two monkeys in front of the theatre. Their owner sets a cake of gingerbread on a painted pole, and they scamper up to the top to search for it."

For a moment I forgot where I was, it was like the old days in our garret when I had acted out a scene for Martin; I held up my hand as if I were begging for a groat, I imitated the children tugging each other by the sleeve, and the chattering, victorious monkey dropping crumbs on to an old washerwoman's head. Ursula laughed, I scratched my shoulder, and hopped most piteously, until there was a noise behind me. The two gentlemen had come back into the room.

"Thou art nothing but an ape thyself," Mr Beaumont laughed, "and I would I had a tester to spare thee, but thine own Londoners rejected my comedy and so thou canst have a cake in the kitchen, but no silver. But listen, boy, though thou art not to speak of it to any save thy master, I have an idea for a new play, and mayhap there will be a part in it for thee. Take this paper to Mr Sly, and tell him to wait for me about sunset at the *Dragon*. And," he added, as I made my legge to them, "stop stuffing thy head with those ridiculous ballads."

"If Mr Beaumont had enough angels in his purse to stage a masque, he would never write a line for us players." Mr Sly looked up reproachfully, as if he expected me to dispute the matter, but I remained dutifully silent.

"We are here on a wild goose chase, though his friend, Mr Fletcher, swears he has a play in his closet; still, I am glad of a breath of country air, after my last ague, I hate the very smell of my chamber."

"It has been a long winter," I ventured.

"Long! Fie on thee, thou art young, thou hast no cares."

I stared at the empty road that ran in front of the *Green Dragon,* and, for the tenth time that evening, crushed down the words that rose to my lips. What was youth to me? Only a time of loneliness. I could never forgive myself for my betrayal of Martin. Oh, my comrade had been kind, he had taken me to the wharf where my boat for London was waiting, on the following morning, and had tried to ease the smart of my cowardice. "Look, Sands, 'tis not thy fault that this city life has so softened thee. Perhaps it is for the best. I should hate to see my own playfellow tumble into the waves." The summer had dragged itself to a close, autumn had come, I had hoped and prayed that Martin would bound into the kitchen shouting, "Sands, where art thou? I am back again." But there had been no news, and although a few old sailors on the Bankside thought that the *Seagull* might be wintering abroad, I knew in my heart that my companion would never return.

To add to my guilt, I had gained advancement from the incident. I was Mother Crofton's favourite now, she often slipped an extra slice on to my trencher, whispering, as she did so, "This is for my sister's sake." Even Mr Sly had said, "What, Sands! Back to time! Thou art growing up, and we must find thee a part or two." Yet my dreams turned sour, and I tossed from side to side before I could sleep at night, knowing that I had failed to grasp the opportunity that had been given to me. Then, because it was easier to work than to brood, I had become more skilful at my craft, but again, at the very instant that I understood a line or mastered some

movement, I caught the eyes of the company watching Mr
Sly, and my future turned to fear once more. There was no
place for a boy whose master was ailing, and for all his gaiety
when he strode across the wooden planks in his slashed velvet
doublet, Sly was less nimble every season. The ague had him
by the bones, and he was increasingly irritable and difficult.

I jumped, as a figure turned the corner. "Here is Mr
Beaumont, sir," I said, and handed my master his cloak.

"And about time too, I am parched for want of some sack.
Who does he think he is, thus to keep his betters waiting? I'll
tell thee, boy, he is a landless younger son, with a pretty wit
at times, and when he chooses, merry. But we have to watch
him, boy, and prune his lines. You can jest at the citizens,
even, within measure, at their wives; but woe to whoever flips
a word at those brawling flat tops, the prentices, and as for
a worshipful grocer, if you as much as smile in his direction,
you'll be lucky to escape with a fine and not closure."

I remembered the disaster of the watchet slops, and
nodded. It was whispered among us boys that Mr Sly had
been dissuaded with difficulty from having the sleeves of his
spring doublet made of primrose satin. In the dark reds, or
soft ash colours, favoured by the older players, he looked like
a knight from some ambassador's train; instead, he insisted
upon wearing the pale greens or light blues that a youth
selected to show that he was first in love.

"Give you good even, Mr Sly." It was like the crying of

the hour upon a holiday morning to hear that deep voice again. "Since I met with you last, I have uncovered the skeleton of a play, but the jade needs substance, she is all bone and no flesh. Yet if I fatten her upon the very grass of Parnassus, what assurance have I that your solemn-pated Londoners will not chase her from the stage?"

"Mr Fletcher says, at the Blackfriars . . ."

"Go to! Mr Fletcher says! 'Tis only an excuse to draw me back to the Bankside before my pocket is ready for it. The country is a quiet mistress. She decks herself with daffodils and does not ask me even for a ribbon."

"Nor, good sir, has she deprived you of wit. But if it please you, Mr Beaumont, let us go inside for some wine. This air to you may be merely a light breeze, but I smell ague in it."

"Nay, Mr Sly, I should be loath to add to your suffering." I held the door open, and they disappeared into the *Dragon* without as much as a look in my direction. I could only catch a phrase or two amid the confusion of voices. "What do I lack?" That was Beaumont's laughter, then I missed the next sentence because Sly was shouting for the drawer, and heard next, ". . . spring suit, because you would not have me appear before you in last season's doublet!" There were footsteps, the sound of a chair being moved, ". . . and twelvepence for the ordinary." Then the innkeeper shut the door again and left me alone with my thoughts.

I went back to the bench and sat down. It was a warm, soft evening, although it was still early in the year. Londoners were beginning to grumble in the taverns, that even a good player could not make them merry if all he had in his mouth was a speech that they had heard since they were babes. "The day of the great tragedy is over," Sly had declared throughout the winter to whoever would listen to him. "Oh, perhaps a Roman one is still possible, with plenty of processions and songs, but the people are tired. Life is hard, and they would rather see the young man get his love, instead of the greybeard, although this, if you reflect upon it, is as fantastic a fable as any tale of the Barbary kings; or else they want a witty clown to jigge them the lastest news, barely this side of the law."

It was true that there was less desire for learning and advancement than in my childhood. Men talked about the insidious danger of the Spaniards in our midst, but nobody did anything about them. Perhaps it was disappointment. Too much had happened during the past twenty years, war, rebellion, the voyages of discovery. Some citizens had said that the old Queen could not hold the reins of government firmly enough in her fingers; everything would change, there would be fresh meaning in all lives, once we had a King again. Then the King had come, and with him the Scots, and after them, the taxes. We seemed to be suffering from some intermittent fever, not dangerous in itself but able to spread a blight across the days, so that nothing seemed completely the right colour, and the only men left with zest were our enemies, the Puritans. "We want something new, something to remind us of youth," Sly would continue, thumping the table beside him, while I had thought, watching the first lonely catkins in our neighbour's garden, that he was old, and that both he and his fellows were living in the past.

I looked up at the rough, green monster painted on the inn sign swinging above my head, and wished that I might join the pair inside. If life could be altered in a moment, as some said, mine had been transformed by Mr Beaumont in the woods that morning. He had broken some leash that had been holding back my thoughts, and tossed adventure like a ball to me. With him no speculation was forbidden; and the wonder and the danger of this swept through my blood till my mouth was full of the taste of crab apples, that are sharp and yet doubly sweet, being the last fruit of the year. I leaned back against the wall, a little drowsily because I had been out in the air all day, and thought of the manor and its orchard, orderly and quiet, after the shouting watermen or the howling of tormented beasts around the Beargarden and the wharves. How could I leave this happiness and return to Southwark next day? Yet I had to obey my master. If I were free, I thought, if I were free... then I suppose that I fell asleep, because the dusk was changing into darkness when my master called me, and Mr Beaumont was fastening his cloak, ready to depart. "If you can spare him, let him stay"; both looked at me, and I realised that I was the object of their conversation. "The mischievous imp rests me with his merry prattle, and he can ride to London with me when I return, three weeks come Thursday."

"With the play?" Sly asked. This was more important at the moment than his prentice.

"Yes, with the play. That is," and Beaumont smiled at me, "if the nymphs of the woods still bless my thoughts."

"We need something new," Sly grumbled. "They laugh at the pastorals they used to applaud, and the countryman fresh from Wales."

"No, not new," Mr Beaumont spoke so gravely that my master at first missed the jest behind the words, "what you want are old bones and new trappings."

"Old bones!" Sly was quick to take offence, and his hand went to his belt. "Oh, I understand you, good sir," he straightened his ruff, "You mean that, like wine, an old comedy is better, but with new words and fresh tricks."

"There is also the place. A great declamation, fit for the wind to mew at, might blow out the candles at Blackfriars."

"It is not for me to dispute your learned judgement, Mr Beaumont, but audiences are alike, wherever they happen to sit. They like a play to follow the same pattern, of wrongs righted and virtue triumphant."

"Like a tilt yard, with two knights evenly matched; but there is no Gloriana now to crown the victors."

"Those were good days. There was more laughter, and people spoke their minds more readily; still," Sly shrugged his shoulders, "as long as we amuse the rascals and get their silver, what is it to us if the folk sitting there be honest fools or not?"

"Alas, Mr Sly, that is true. Agreed, I will do my best for you. It will be an old play, because my masters are the Latins, and I am not so foolish as to think that I can surpass them. But it will be new as well. The conception of it labours mightily; 'twill be a sad tale, but very gallant." His fingers twitched as if he longed to return to his tablets. "And can I have the boy?" he added, as an afterthought.

"You are welcome to him. The wag was a good nurse to me during the winter, and deserves a holiday. Besides, unless he soon runs off some of my housekeeper's generous dinners, his belly will burst his doublet, and I shall have to buy him a new one."

"Then send him up to the manor tomorrow morning." Mr Beaumont bowed as if he were taking leave of a fellow courtier, while Sly responded, for all his training, a little awkwardly. "My salutations to your fellows, and may God grant you a good journey." Before I had time to run and thank him, he was halfway up the road.

"Boy!" Sly called, and as I knelt to babble words of gratitude, he tweaked my ear. "Didst thou see how he saluted me? Verily, I might have been King James himself! Keep thy wits about thee, and watch how he moves. That is why I am lending thee to him for a month; it will teach thee how to act a gallant, after thou art grown."

The daffodils had gone, but a King's guard, those marsh lilies, stood stiffly, the length of the stream. I sat on the tree once more, and marvelled at my good fortune. Ever since Master Awsten had died, I had longed to be a page, and live in some quiet and clean manor. Now I knew that the reality was more wonderful than the dream. Mr Beaumont had never had such service. I felt his moods (and they were many), if he needed a cloak, when a book had to be replaced on its shelf, or when he was tired of writing and would have me take a stool and listen to the tale of Perseus. This was the first afternoon that he had sent me out alone. "'Twill do thee more good to ramble than to mope over thy lines," and he had continued, because we were to read his new play that evening to some neighbours, "yes, with good will and a couple of candles, we can make a passable Blackfriars out of this somewhat dilapidated hall, nor need we ask our audience for silver, other than their own imaginations."

The water was still, each separate blade of grass was greener than its fellow, the moss made a Turkey carpet of the stone below me, then I heard a rustling in the bushes, and looked up. "Mistress Ursula!" I said in surprise, "what do you here?"

She had more liberty than our London maids, but was never suffered to leave the garden, without a serving woman to attend her.

"I have waited weeks to see this famous pool where Mr Beaumont comes to meditate, but thou knowest how it is with him, he is either with my father or with his books. As at least a dozen neighbours are coming to supper, my mother has gone herself into the kitchen. I believe she is making us one of her famous possets. So I slipped away to walk a little in the orchard. Thou hast often heard," and she sighed, "how much I like shelling peas!"

I stood up, a little embarrassed, hoping that Mr Beaumont would not think that I had proposed the escapade, and she sat down on the log. "Is it really here that he comes when he is melancholy?" she asked, and when I nodded, added, "'Tis a dark place. I prefer the meadows, and the sun."

"You should have seen it in the spring, when there were only young leaves on the branches."

The light dappled her dress that was itself a field of flowers, and I felt strangely troubled as I waited beside her. "Tell me about the play tonight," she commanded, "Francis... Mr Beaumont... jokes about it, he says it is all moonlight."

I hesitated; all that I had ever felt was in it, my love, my brief glory with my first master, Awsten, the long, innocent playtime with poor Martin. "It is so beautiful that I am afraid of it," I stammered.

"Afraid! Why, Sands, how is it possible for beauty to frighten thee?"

"Because it is ... how shall I explain it ... the full sensation of a moment. Mostly we live in memory, but this is like the story that Mr Beaumont told us, the other evening. Do you remember, about the boy and the eagle? We are lifted up, we cannot apprehend where fate is taking us, it stretches our senses until we lose our grip, and drop. It can never be again, and yet it never ends."

"I can see that thou art a poet, like my master."

"I! No!" I defended myself vehemently, "I am too fond of pies."

Yet there was something that separated me from my fellows. I had a gift, though I could not explain what it was. It could not be fantasy alone, because it was something that I had recognised in the grave mariner face of Martin's uncle as much as in the melancholy of Mr Beaumont. It was unpredictable, it fell as unexpectedly on its votaries as thistledown; people who did not have it were indifferent, because it was outside the bounds of their experience, but it was in the words that I was to speak that night, and in the way that Ursula's eyes were following a yellow butterfly as it flew across the water. "I should like to pen verses, it is true," I said, "but they do not even limp with me, they hop."

"Like fleas!" Ursula suggested, and we both laughed. She even jumped on one foot, very prettily, over to the stream and back. "Tell me the story of the play," she begged, sitting down again on the old log.

"Alas, I may not, I swore an oath to Mr Beaumont."

"A poet's oath, a lover's oath," she mocked.

"Wait," I said, brushing off a cobweb that had stuck to her skirt, "it is to be a surprise. You will hear it all in a few hours."

"Hast a part to thy liking?" she asked innocently. "Mr Beaumont told us that he will read the Prince."

"Now I see that my lord has told you the plot already, and you would have had me forsworn for a jest."

"Indeed he has not," she shook her head indignantly, "we only know that there is to be a princess in it, because young Bruford, the one we laugh at because if our old mastiff is loose, he is afraid to cross the yard, asked my mother for the loan of a headdress. He told her that he was to play a wronged lady."

"He has the complexion," I said, with some annoyance. The fellow had tried to treat me as if I were a barefooted clown, and then had minced and simpered as if he had been lady in waiting to Queen Anne herself. "But we are only reading the play tonight," I added, "not acting it."

"'Twill seem like acting to me, who have never been inside a playhouse. I wish I could accompany Mr Beaumont. Ah me, 'tis sad to be a maid."

"After you are married," I said politely, "perhaps Mr

Beaumont will take you to Blackfriars. The other houses are too turbulent for a lady." I thought with disgust of the drunken jests and brawling on the Bankside.

"Married! Sometimes I am afraid." She clutched the leaf-embroidered panel of her dress, as I had often been scolded for doing when a skirt got in my way. "Mr Beaumont lives by himself in the upper air. I brought him a rose from the garden the other morning, and he gazed at it as if it were the very globe itself; then that same night he asked me indifferently at dinner whether I cared for flowers. They might have been nettles to him, or weeds!"

"He pours all he has into the moment. Afterwards he does not remember. It is a form of exhaustion."

"Does it happen to thee as well?" Ursula asked curiously.

"Oh no, whenever I want to fly, the earth sticks to my heels."

"Yes, a ballad or a story will go round and round in my head, as if it were happening in front of me; then Patience calls me to help her in the kitchen, and alack, in a moment, not a thread of it is left."

"I have never known anyone as remote as Mr Beaumont."

"If he is thinking about plays, I am only uneasy lest I should disturb him; but, Sands, he makes such jests about the Court! Suppose one of his companions should denounce him?"

I could not reply, because this same fear had been running through my own head.

"He says that the times are evil, and it is true. Most of the beggars round the market place are soldiers back from Flanders. But he mocks at the justices, and they are powerful."

"The gods and the Muses will protect him," I murmured, but without much conviction.

"He says so himself. He is always talking about a wisdom higher than our law. He says that if we believe in it, it will shield us."

"Oh, Perseus," I said, and Ursula looked at me enquiringly.

"It is a story about a voyage. A Greek sailor went searching for the herb of truth. After he had found it, he showed it to people, and they died. But there is a cordial in the Indies that is said to cure the plague."

"He likes sad tales. But dost thou really think that there is any remedy against great sickness?"

"Perhaps. I told you the other afternoon about my comrade, Martin. The Indians cured him of a violent fever in a few hours."

"I am so frightened of the plague." Perhaps it was the shadowy light, but the flowers on her bodice seemed to shiver.

"And so am I." I thought of the rasping sound the death cart made on the stones, and how I stuffed my head under the cover trying not to listen to it. "My father died of it," I said. "He was buried before a messenger could reach me."

Another yellow butterfly settled on a stump beside us. I heard the faint splash of a water rat among the reeds.

We were far away from the white, unhealthy dust that the pack horses kicked up as they went by, or the noises and commotion of a city street. "The Kentish air is pure," Ursula murmured, "but this is only a visit. Mr Beaumont dwells, as thou knowest, in London. He told me about thy father." She caught my sleeve to show me a bird rising up from the marsh lilies, and a strange thing happened. I forgot that I was a player's boy, and took her hand, as if I had been really some squire's son. I was neither shy nor indifferent, as I commonly was with maids. She did not move, but said, pointing to the opposite bushes, "Oh, I almost wish I were a babe again, when every gorse blossom was a golden galleon, and tragedy was to drop my ginger-bread doll into the pond."

"And I am glad that you are not," I said, and smiled at her very confidently.

"Why, Sands!" She looked up in surprise.

"If you were a babe, I should have to carry you home, and you would pull my hair, and forget me tomorrow. As it is, I shall pretend this is a holiday." To make her laugh, I made the clumsy legge that a stable boy would use, and clutched my cap with both hands. "Will it please you to walk in the woods with me, sweet mistress?" I do not know what scruple prevented me from taking her in my arms.

"Now give me leave, sir knave, I am not thy Joan,"

she sang back at me from a harvest round.

"But I have a fairing," I said, and I offered her a stalk of shadow grass, as solemnly as if I had jolted back from market on a carter's pony.

"And thou hast put on a clean shirt! Not for me, but because it is Saturday."

We both laughed, and then I saw her glance up the stream as if to take farewell of it. "Come, Sands, thou must show me the best way to the manor. If my mother finds out that I have played truant, she will lock me in my room. I should miss the play, and Mr Beaumont would be angry. Besides, I should weep my eyes out for a week."

The room was almost dark. A rough platform had been knocked together at the end of the hall, and we were ready to begin, as soon as the candles were arranged to Mr Beaumont's liking. I had never known him so gay nor so patient. A spot of wax had fallen on his fine velvet doublet, but instead of reproving the servingman, he had made the incident into a jest, bidding me tell Mr Sly that he had thus paid his admission fees, and was duly a member of our craft. I looked down at the double circle of people sitting in the lower part of the chamber, but it was a moment or two before I saw Ursula. She was on a low stool, next to her father, and talking to him eagerly. It must have been the flickering candlelight, but instead of my gay companion of the afternoon, I saw a young nobleman, walking round the battlements of a

castle during our civil wars. It was only a flash, I could not
discover whether he wore the white rose or the red, but the
gold cord glittered in his black velvet cap, and faded fields,
the colour of a gillyflower, stretched from the walls towards
the hills. We could have been comrades in arms, I thought
in bewilderment, and nobody would have questioned my
degree. Then Ursula moved her head; as she answered some
whispered comment of her father, the impression vanished;
I felt the hard knots of the boards under my feet, and longed
for her to be beside me, in place of that gull, young Bruford,
who was going to read the part of Arethusa. I was almost
angry with my own imagination (though it was probably the
figures in the threadbare arras, hanging on the wall); I had
no use today for images from the past. I wanted this hour,
this something that had never been before, and would never
be again, until I heard an echo mocking me, "Youth, boy, all
you said you did not want."

Some of Mr Beaumont's friends had come with their
viols; he nodded to them, and the music began. I wished
that I had dared to whisper to Ursula, before we had parted
in the evening dusk, "Mark the story, it is almost my own."
Bellario had loved Philaster, but because of the difference
in rank she had followed him disguised as a country page.
So Awsten had found me; and in almost a repetition of
the incident, Mr Beaumont had encountered me, sitting
upon a log beside the stream. Philaster had given his boy

to Arethusa whom he loved, as Awsten had had to give me up to Mr Sly. I am Bellario, I thought, as Mr Beaumont rose to read his part, with a slow, beautiful motion as if the globe were his plaything, and his lines, the air. Love was service, and sometimes I did not know which of the two I most wanted to be with; but tonight I was swept by an over-mastering desire, I wanted to take Ursula back into the hazardous woods and show her that I could be as wild and ardent as my master. It was then that I remembered her mother's voice, earlier in the evening. "How well young Bruford looks in that coif that I lent him! You can tell that he is a gentleman's son, in spite of his mumming, which is more than you can say of most of the company." I tried to pretend that she meant the stable boy, who had been pressed indoors to make the riot noises at the beginning of the fifth act, or the neighbour's third son who was shouting Pharamond's speeches as if he were some reveler, from the *Dragon*, stumbling homeward through the night; but I knew in my heart that she had included me, I was not gentle by blood, however softly I might speak and no matter what service I might render to the squire.

Yet what ultimately was this degree? The sun moved from one patch of meadow to another, but the grasses grew the same on both, although at a different time. It was neither land nor gifts that were important, but how we used them; why should we be kennelled into squares, as if life were the checkerboard of a universe incapable of change? I wanted to fly with Mr Beaumont, to be fluid, to rise, to come to golden answers falling from the sun, and sweep forward with the new, grand tide into motion and discovery. Somebody touched my arm, my scene was about to begin, but as I stepped forward I did not see Ursula in the semi-circle of darkness. Instead I heard a whisper mocking me again, "Sands, fellow, I know more about thee than thou thinkest, why didst thou leave me; in the Indies all are equal."

Time raced, because we were reading the scenes, and not acting them. Pity me, I prayed to Fortune, I am no counterfeit page, this is myself speaking, or that other, shadowy being in me, that I do not always recognise. We became absorbed into the pattern of the verse; phrase, movement and feeling fused into one, until the whole act glowed like the ruby that Prince Henry had worn on his helmet, riding in procession through London. My coldness could melt; until Mr Beaumont had given me the words I had not known that I was lonely. I, too, could conquer this stubborn art that until now had eluded me. We saw in dream, but hearing was the more immediate, it was the present compared with the past; yes, speech needed its own interpreters because few seemed to be aware of it, yet it had the power of flying, it could carry the ears above any murmur of the lute players, into the silence that was more important than the sound. And suddenly (although it was again the light upon the very

worn arras) two gold doors swung ajar in front of me, opening slowly, shutting once more, both of them the colour of
sunlight moving with the wind. Beyond them was Helicon,
the new motions of the mind, the great masque that was
outside our mortal limitations. Then, just as I was about to
pass the gates, the unpractised player King stumbled over his
two final lines, the walls became solid, Mr Beaumont saluted
the circle with a wide sweep of his hat, and the audience
started to applaud, quietly at first as if they were still a little
dazed, and lustily afterwards, as if we were at a hunt.

It was over. The glory was ended. They had listened to
Bellario but not to me, whatever we had made was in an
eternity of its own, it was not here. People pressed towards
Mr Beaumont, and the squire's son, his coif under his arm,
minced over to his friends with the assurance of a practised
player. He had been the only one to dress in costume for the
performance. "It ended just in time," a servingman grumbled, coming in with fresh candles. "Another minute, and
the room would have been in darkness. Not that the ladies
would have taken that amiss," he added in a rough whisper. The door was flung open; the old mastiff that had been
shut up in the pantry lest he should snore came bounding in
to snuffle round his master. "Will there be enough stools?"
somebody queried. "Wait a moment, we can get the bench
out of the tool shed." A blue-coated servingman, lent by a
neighbour, marched through the room towards the dining

hall, carrying a huge platter of beef, and the younger men started to applaud him.

"It was a sad, pitiful tale," the lady beside me murmured. "It reminded me of my first love. I would I were fourteen again."

"Go to! By waiting a year thou hadst a knight of the shire, and thine own coach." We all smiled at these indignant words, because the speaker's ruff had wilted in the heat, and her stomacher was so pointed that she resembled the top half of a painted, wooden giant rather than a sober matron.

"All the same, he was a proper young man, and he died in Flanders," the first woman affirmed, dabbing her eyes. "I remember..."

"Nay, good my lady, memories are dangerous." It was the fat squire speaking, who was so famous for his hounds. "Yesterday is past, think instead of the posset that I see them bearing to the upper table. For my part, watching a play is a whet stone for my appetite. I'd as soon hunt otters till my boots were full of water, than sit on a stool for hours, listening to a tale I cannot follow."

"'Twas a sweet child that played the page, though a trifle solid looking."

"But to speak of riots, in these times! And against princes of the blood. Dost think..." My neighbour dropped his voice and muttered something that I could not hear.

"Nay, calm yourself, good sir." His companion shook

his head. "Whatever he may think in his study, our friend Beaumont is too witty a gentleman to jeopardise his freedom by a foolish word. Besides, I know these writers. What we have heard tonight is hot from his fancy, now he will send the piece to the players to be schooled."

I shivered in spite of this reassurance. The world was upside down, as the broadsheets said, and a jest today could lead as easily to gaol as laughter. People whispered that Ralegh was imprisoned in the Tower because he was Lady Arabella's champion, and she, in turn, was confined to a country estate, forbidden to marry or to come to Court. Yet although I had collected the pages of the play as fast as Mr Beaumont had written them, I knew no more than the squire's mastiff about his political ideas, nor whether some deeper current ran beneath this apparently harmless story of young love.

The groups dispersed. I followed them out respectfully, tasting the disappointment in my mouth; it was not salt as people said, but like lukewarm water on a flat, thundery day. Ursula had disappeared, although I could see her mother's white hair above the throng of bright silks, but I stopped at the door, hoping desperately for I knew not what, while I looked round for my master. "Quick, Sands," one of our own servitors called, hurrying past me with an armful of dishes, "they have kept a trencher of beef for thee in the kitchen, but the spit boy will eat it an thou lingerest here." Flagons banged on the board, another servant cursed at me for standing in his way, but I should have gone on watching the assembly had a voice not shouted, "Where's my boy?"

"Here, sir." I looked up to see Mr Beaumont smiling down at me.

"Good, Sands, I've brought thee a sprig of rosemary for thy cap, there being no laurel by," and he winked, "and no sixpences either." Then he clapped me lightly on the cheek and added, "Now go eat thy meat, before the larder is swept bare. For once thou hast deserved it."

The herb garden was the sunniest spot in all Kent. I had left a token beside the lavender bush to show Ursula where I was, several white pebbles in the shape of a wing, then I had sat down on a flat slab on top of the low stone wall, and in the drowsy stillness had almost fallen asleep.

What a spring it was! The earliest joys of childhood had returned to me, and this time I had wit enough to recognise and hold them. I had never known such a holiday! There were no beatings, no smells, and I slept alone in a small room, free to dream with neither a kick nor a snore to disturb the night, until the morning light called me into the fields. For weeks the household had spoiled me, from the old cook who had left sugar comfits beside my truckle bed, to the factor who had taken me riding with him round the farms. I had learned the number of logs we could expect to cut out of an old tree, and how to measure seed for a long, irregular field. There was Thursday to come, that black, terrible day when Mr Beaumont would return to London, but meantime it was treason to think about it, to miss one moment of this glorious, godlike time, with the bees humming, the flowers opening, and all the people gentle. Oh, how the world would change if everyone were kind!

I picked a blade of wind-sown grass from a crevice between the stones, the doves called to each other, the air smelt of fresh grass; then I heard a voice at the wicket gate. "Alas, Patience, the hem of my apron has come undone, I pray thee, fetch me my smock from the hook in my room." I ducked between two bushes, until I saw the rim of the maid's straw hat vanish round the stable corner, and then hurried forward down the path.

"Give thee good morrow, Sands, I thought I should find thee here."

"I have been waiting for an hour, Mistress Ursula, but I knew that with Mr Beaumont present, you would sit longer at table."

"What wit he has! It transforms my father into the courtier that he must have been before I was born, and dazzles my mother so that she cannot speak. Yet I am not amazed that Mr Beaumont is often melancholy, it must be a burden to see so clearly through fools."

"He uses learning as other men use wine. It brings with it a great fatigue."

"He jests about the Court until I tremble and my mother frowns, and will mimic you a raw, Scottish knight coming into Whitehall in so droll a manner that we have to laugh with him. Then, while the clumping and the stammering is still in our ears, he will rise above the best preacher that I ever heard, discoursing of the liberty of the mind in what he calls the fettered subject. And finally, after we are dazed from so much contemplation, down we come to earth again, with a tragi-comical tale of a woodcutter who lost his purse at market to some city rascal who pretended to be a liveried servant. Only it shatters my weak mind, I am fain to sit on the ground and pick daisies." Her skirt brushed my knees, as she climbed up beside me on the wall.

"You can talk to me, I am all earth, I was never further in my studies than orthography."

"He says he will teach me Latin when we marry. Sometimes a word slips into his speech of such beauty that it is a madrigal in itself, but I, poor wretch, do not know if he is telling me about a river or a nymph, and am too timid to ask."

"And he mocks me for what he calls my love of a three-penny ballad, but we are English, not Roman."

"He declared this noon that virtue was but an accident of circumstance."

"Oh, there he is wrong. I have only to look at you to know the contrary."

"Yet Mr Beaumont declares that thou art tired of us, and count the moments till thy return to London."

"I! Tired! A thousand times no! When that day comes I shall hide myself in the woods."

"But thou must miss thy companions, and the brave shows in the streets; come now, confess thou wilt be glad to see them."

I shook my head, I could smell the stale air of the garret and hear the grumbling voices shouting for me. "You do not know, Mistress Ursula, what the life of an apprentice is. I want only to remain at the manor."

"Poor child!" Ursula said a little mockingly, "but what wouldst thou do, without thy craft?"

"I would I could be your page."

Ursula glanced up the path to see if Patience was returning with the smock. "Alas, that is impossible."

"I know. Dr Bentwood has told us in a hundred sermons that it is our duty to stay within our degree, but I do not believe him. We give more to our fellows when we are happy."

Ursula slid down from the wall as if she had heard the sound of footsteps. I thought that she looked puzzled. "The company has spent money on me," I pleaded, "they have a right to be repaid. But my master is ill, and has often said he is not well enough to train me. If Mr Beaumont took me, it would not cost him much, and I would serve him without wages until the last sixpence was returned to him."

"Listen, Sands, I should not say this to you, I know." (I started when she used the formal address, as if I were some cousin's son, and not a servant.) "But we love the same things, the sun, this garden, the jokes we have had with each other. It is not a question of money but the world. Our elders, alas, do not see life with our eyes. The village gossips say that you are fond of me. You are young enough, this summer, so that they can laugh, and that is your safety, at what seems to them a natural and amusing folly. Another year, it would not be the village but my kinsmen. My mother has bidden me already not to treat you as a playmate."

"I know that you are to marry Mr Beaumont. I never asked more than to serve you both as master and mistress. Call what I feel loyalty, and not love."

"Alas, Sands, it cannot be. This is a boon that I may not ask Mr Beaumont, nor must you fret if I am distant with you at our next meeting."

"It was too like heaven to last," I said, and as I spoke we heard Patience step on to the cracked, uneven tile in front of the stable door.

"Be brave, Sands, there is the play, your play..." I felt lips brush my cheek, but it was the kiss of a child; then Ursula ran down the path crying a little too vehemently, as if she suspected that the maid might report our meeting to her mother if she saw us, "No, Patience, no, not that heavy thing, it is too hot, but no matter, my father has sent for me. He bids me join him immediately in the hall."

"Sands!"

"Yes, Mr Beaumont."

"Heaven protect us, boy, from such a gesture! Euphrasia is a gently nurtured maid. Think of Mistress Ursula, and don't stamp."

"I crave your pardon," I moaned. I knew as well as Mr Beaumont that every movement I was making was wrong, but something had happened to me. It was not only the shock of leaving Sundridge and all that the manor had meant to me, but also too much repetition. I could no more breathe life into the lines than a rabbit could change its ears.

"Again! Oh, God be with us, wilt thou drive me out of my wits? Make thy supplication without wringing thy fingers, or I'll go get Rice to take thy place."

"'Tis in the book."

"What book?"

"The one on the art of gesture." We had slaved over the motion for a week, thumbs slightly bent and fingers outstretched. Rice had christened it the "ball catcher," and we had laughed so much that we had been given dry bread for supper as a punishment. "It is a true translation from the Italian," I added.

"But thou art an English youth! And what do our worshipful citizens know of Padua or Venice? They will whistle, and pelt thee with their orange skins. Put thy paws behind thy back, and start again."

I had only to plead with Philaster in the scene as I was now pleading with my master in real life, but the words would not come; I mispronounced one, and stopped.

"Try to remember that day when we sat together on a log to make a posy," Mr Beaumont said patiently. "Here, take this for a flower, if thou canst not see it in thy head," and he thrust his quill into my hands.

"But my scene is in a palace," I said stupidly.

"Sands, Sands, art lunatic thyself? This is the preparation. Thou hast to make thine audience perceive what is only to be spoken later, in another scene. The happiest moment of my page's life was when Philaster took him from the fountain; the unhappiest, the day that his master handed him over to the Princess, proving, young sir, that with one flash of his green eyes, madman Love wipes out loyalty and service and all good works." Mr Beaumont snatched back the quill, walked across to a little table, and scribbled a line on his tablets; then he came back to the stool beside me, and smiled, "Lucky child, thou hast not felt the galling of his yoke."

"I have," I said. The weeks since I had last seen Ursula seemed a lifetime of years.

"No, not the madness. Else I had not chosen thee for

this part. Look, boy, I'll give thee an apple as salve for thy throat, if only thou wilt say those opening lines aright."

The floor of the room was thick with dust, in the attic above us a man was practising on the viol, there were cart wheels rumbling over the cobbles outside. Everything was clear and sharp, but I, in the middle of it, was empty and brittle, the straw after the barley had been reaped.

"Forget what thou hast learned," Mr Beaumont continued, "let them feel the words from the throat and not the belly; keep thy head up, and don't rant."

"I cannot do it," I said flatly. "It won't come."

"It will, with a good beating. I'll stop thy pies and thy Sunday rambles. What has got into thee, boy; it was Bellario himself speaking, in Kent."

Oh, but then Ursula was listening to me, I wanted to reply. It had been easy with the candlelight falling on a single board, and the darkness round us. The words had made their own life, disconnected from what I was; the applause had not been mine, it had belonged to the figures upon the arras, no, to the gods that were behind them.

"'Tis the loveliest poetry that ever was penned, but I cannot say it."

"I believe it is not mere obstinacy, boy," Mr Beaumont looked at me thoughtfully, "but the part should speak itself, and thou art strangling it."

"It is because it is so beautiful…"

"Is it the London crowd that frightens thee, or thine own fellows?"

The day that Mr Beaumont had asked for me, Taylor had whistled. "Take Rice," he had suggested, "Sands is perilous uncertain." I should have jumped into the Thames if they had taken Bellario away from me, but Mr Beaumont had answered immediately, "Oh, I owe a fragment of a scene to the wag, let him have his chance." He had even persuaded them to let him rehearse me first himself. There had been jeers and whisperings, "Answer me this riddle, *mistress* Sands," our master of fence had flung at me, in front of my companions. "What goes first out of the casement in the morning? A nobleman's fancy, or the reckoning from last night's dinner?" I had sprung at him with my baited weapon, and though he had disarmed me in a second, he had patted my head. "So, so, I see my little mastiff has a good thrust in tierce if provoked. Speak him gently, and he falls asleep." Yet it was not the other prentices but a complete severance from emotion that made my world shallow. It was less suffering itself than an all-pervading greyness. "I suppose," I mumbled, "it is the hopelessness of life."

"Thou hast a craft, food in thy belly, and good friends. Take thy choice, boy, gold or philosophy, there's nothing else. So master thy surroundings, that is the wise man's first lesson. And now, sir scholar," Mr Beaumont smiled at me very kindly, "start that speech again. Shift thy love from thy liver to thy throat, and watch thy hands. Thou art here to plead with thy master," he mocked the gesture of entreaty so gaily with his own hands that I had to laugh, "and not to gather nuts."

"Art ready, Sands?"

I nodded. It was hard beyond endurance but I must cease to be myself; only if I detached myself from my surroundings would the words come out, as lightly as thoughts.

"Thou art quite the gallant in that page's suit."

Mr Beaumont had bought the clothes from a courtier whose son had attended a wedding. I had seldom had such velvet in my hands, let alone on my back, yet it might have been fustian for all that it mattered to me. I dared not think of my appearance, or I should stand up presently stiffer than a painted ninepin, ready to be knocked over by a ball or the crowd.

"Rub thy cheeks, boy, rub thy cheeks. Thou hast been a prentice long enough not to be frightened."

"The other plays meant nothing to me," I stammered.

"The more shame to thee and to thy craft."

"But the populace has no judgement," I pleaded. "They will stamp at the best scene ever penned because they are out of humour, and sob like frantic monkeys at some melancholic folly."

"Speak thy part as it was spoken once in Kent, and thou
wilt have no cause to be alarmed."

A circle of light, smaller than the smallest ring, began to
revolve in my head. The terror was lifting. There would be
neither eggs to spoil my velvet nor epithets to irritate my
temporary master. The courtiers would drink to him, he would
be their "rare wit" and gentle companion. Even I should have
my crumb of praise, and yet I knew, oh, why must I see this
so clearly, that I should never repeat this single illumination.
They would weep at my words, but I should not be speaking
them. No, Fate had caught me up in one of her designs, and
would drop me after the evening were finished, it mattered
not whether harshly or softly, because her real concern was not
with me but with this figure in his magnificent new maiden-
hair-brown and silver doublet, standing patiently beside me.
"I have the vision," I said, "I have the vision...."

"I care not what thou hast, an my play is a success. I am
as weary as thou art of their yowling and bawling. Now they
have got everything they want, from the wronged princess
and her love-sick hero, to the greedy suitor with a bawdy
mistress. An thou failest me tonight, I'll have thee whipped
every supper time for a week."

"I cannot help being afraid."

"Thou art trained to know thy craft. No more of this
nonsense." He took me by the shoulder, and shook me. The
ice seemed to melt, my tongue loosened, and the first lines

that I had to speak in the play tumbled out of my mouth:

"Sir, you did take me up
When I was nothing; and only yet am something
By being yours."

But I hoped he would understand that these words meant to me — good Mr Beaumont, if I do well, let me be your page, take me back to Sundridge.

"That's better, boy," Beaumont smiled at me as if I were Ursula. "Come," he continued, and we pushed our way out of the tiring room. I could hear the familiar sounds, stools scraping, grumbling, the tuning of viols. *"Oranges, fresh oranges!"* In spite of my resolution, I could not help glancing at my new doublet. It was cold, I began to tremble again, how could a tale of loneliness and love move our assembling audience? What were we other than an interlude between their dinner and a game of dice? Philaster strolled up, with his mouth full of liquorice, pompous-brave in deep blue, to show us his new cloak. Awsten could have calmed me with a glance, but I had never been old enough to play opposite him, except as a serving boy at the back of the stage. This man had no time for me, I was not his pupil. "Look ye!" he said angrily as Beaumont greeted him, and he pointed to a thread on his sleeve, "some impertinent fool has ripped my lace."

"'Tis no matter, there will be no thought of fashion when

you begin to speak." To my amazement, the fellow drank the flattery up as if it had been a glass of Rhenish wine, and smiled at us benignly.

Taylor tweaked my ear, a fellow shouted that the King's chair was missing, a youth passed us with tobacco for his master. The sounds died down, Philaster spread his fingers in the half supplication that was to be his first gesture, looked at them, and then adjusted his cloak. "I hope they have swept the stage," he whispered, "I have to kneel." A man beckoned, and he walked slowly forward, the opening scene had begun.

My own entrance was not until the second act. I knew again so clearly as I waited that a piece of my own life was ending; the more skilfully I played, the more reluctant the company would be to give me up, the more successful the play, the more often Beaumont would sup with his friends, and the less silver he would have to keep a servant. It is unjust, I wanted to scream, but when I looked up at the melancholy face beside me, I remembered that I had vowed obedience to the Muses. Yet I could only think of Kent, the lambs by the stream, Ursula running after her dog, the drowsy evenings after royal days; and then (perhaps Fortune herself pitied me?) my holiday happiness returned, but in a different degree. A storm lifted me suddenly and left me on a distant hill, half suffocated by its power. I must have rubbed my throat, for Beaumont smiled. The sensation was over in an instant, I felt empty and alone, but all fear had gone.

"Thou wilt be whipped, Sands, in spite of thy velvet," Rice whispered, coming up with a most ungirlish flourish of his petticoats, although in a few moments he would make a most pitiful princess.

"You wait till afterwards," I growled, more aggressively than usual, but I knew now that I should not fail.

"Think of the woods," Beaumont said, and pushed me forward. The moment had come, it was even more menacing than I had imagined, but all that I could feel was a slight surprise, as if I were standing still, while the play, the spectators, life itself, swirled round me with an ever increasing motion; then with a craft that I had never previously possessed, I heard myself pleading with my master to keep me in his service (and it was Awsten, Beaumont and Philaster all rolled into one) while beyond, in the half-circle that I felt rather than saw, the coughing ceased and the orange sellers were silent.

IV

"Bred to the King's Service."

October 1618.

HE RAIN PITTED THE DIRTY THAMES. It was a perilous voyage to cross the street, between the deep holes and the almost liquid mud. My old riding boots needed mending; water had come through the soles, and I felt as if I were wading barefoot through the filthy slime. Somebody had stuffed a cloth into a broken pane in the house opposite the *Plough,* the old, solid buildings were in disrepair, trees had been cut down, and gardens neglected. The Southwark of my childhood had almost disappeared. Rubbish heaps soiled the meadows where we used to set our maypoles, and now that the ditches were no longer cleaned, some of the ground was turning back into marsh. Stern necessity kept me to the quarter, and yet, as I counted my few pennies over to make sure that I had enough to pay for a pot of ale, I wondered if I should want to move to London even if an alchemist should change the coins into gold? After the hatred and the turmoil of the early years, Southwark had become all that I had of home. I still slept in the old garret under Mother Crofton's roof; people knew me, and though there were still days when I longed passionately never to see the broken walls and sprawling nettles of the lost gardens again, it was comforting to return after months in the provinces, and hear Mother Crofton call, "I've been airing your bed for you all day," while I was still twenty yards from her door, or have Goodman Humphries, the innkeeper, invite me to drink a health with him in real Bordeaux. Times have changed, I thought, times have changed. We are all poorer, but this is my village, and if I belong anywhere it is here. Yes, Fortune, having robbed me of most of my desires, had tossed my cradle contemptuously back to me. I shook the raindrops from my cloak, scraped off the worst of the mud and hurried into the *Plough*.

"Give you good even, Master Sands," the innkeeper turned from putting some wood on to the fire, "what is your news?"

"Bad," I answered, as soon as I saw that we were alone in the room. "The execution is to be before Westminster Hall, at ten in the morning."

"The poor, brave gentleman," Humphries came forward

and took my cloak himself, "it would have been better for Sir Walter if he had never returned from the Indies."

"I would he had escaped into France."

The water was dripping from my clothes on to the clean, sanded floor. My collar was wet and I could feel how sodden my boots were. "Here, Bess," Humphries called, "take this cloak and dry it in the kitchen. I will heat some sack," he added, "otherwise you may get an ague."

I hardly liked to accept the wine, because the *Plough* these days stood little better with fortune than myself. It had never been one of the great inns, but Master Sly had called it a reasonably quiet place, where a man could talk and drink without a dozen roisterers overturning his table. Now few came in, except from the adjoining streets, hired men who could barely afford a pot of ale, or a Dutch sailor from the colony on the Bankside. The red-cheeked countrywomen of Elizabeth's day, who had first eaten a great pudding, and then had stood in the sun to laugh at the Jigge of the Slippers, now lay in the graveyard. Their mincing daughters lived on possets to keep a fashionable slimness, and preferred a gilt comb to a comedy, even at Blackfriars.

"England is dying," I muttered as Humphries came back with a flagon and two glasses, "they have no use for greatness."

"It's enough to turn the old Queen in her grave. She

liked a proper man who could use his sword, and she had no love for Spain."

"In the old days the apprentices would have risen...."

"And now all they will do is to buy a mournful ballad of the worshipful knight's sad end...."

We sat in silence for a moment, sipping the steaming wine, and I felt my limbs coming to life again. "Wert not afraid to get so wet?" Humphries asked anxiously; he had been my loyal friend throughout all my tribulations. He had scolded me, laughed at me, and then given me as much bread and small beer as I could eat and drink, throughout the many weeks that I had had no money to pay for them. "I never noticed the storm until I came across the bridge," I answered truthfully, "I was thinking about Sir Walter."

The innkeeper nodded. They said that if the Prince had lived, Ralegh would have become second in the realm once more. Henry had praised his wisdom and his desire to found an empire in the Indies, where younger sons might have land, and no man need beg because there was no work for him. "Perhaps there will be a reprieve," Humphries suggested, "a sudden act of clemency?"

I shook my head. "I have little hope of that, because King James is a melancholy lover, without a will of his own when it comes to Spain. He makes a treaty, and afterwards, when our ships sail into Cadiz on their lawful business, our sailors are flung into a Spanish dungeon, and — there they lie still today. He would rather listen to Gondomar than to his Queen. No, this time it is no rehearsal; the tragedy will be played out to its end."

We drew closer to the fire, and neither of us spoke for a few moments; then Humphries looked me up and down, as if he were counting the frayed threads on my right sleeve. "Have you spoken to Master Penny yet?" he asked.

I shook my head. At this particular moment I preferred to put the merchant out of my mind. "Do not delay, boy," Humphries was still staring at my arm, "Dame Fortune is smiling on you at last."

"It's a grave decision to change one livery for another. Suppose I take service with Master Penny, and he dies; I might find myself a beggar on the roads."

"Have no fear, his younger brother is a very worthy gentleman; you would lack neither meat nor drink."

"I am much beholden to you," I murmured, because I knew that Humphries had spoken for me, then I spread my hands out to the blaze. Old Mother Crofton always protested that she could see pictures in the flames, but for all the fantasies that danced round in my head, the hearth looked merely a hearth to me, with the wood crackling and the sparks flying up the chimney. How I wished that I could see the future, as she pretended she could; then my present misgivings would be ended. "The merchant has no reason to reward me," I continued, "I only called for help."

"You saved the gentleman his purse, and it had ten pounds in it. Still, in these times, gratitude is a rare virtue." Humphries reached forward, and put another piece of wood on the fire.

"It used to be the quietest street in Southwark. I know it was rough in the fields over against the bull baiting, but here we were neighbours, loyal to one another."

"And Sir Walter was Captain of the Guard."

"I felt there was mischief about, when that whining bundle of kitchen stuff cringed up to Master Penny. I looked round, and there was Noll, a great stick in his hand, waiting up the alley. So I drew my dagger, and yelled."

"It was fortunate that the Guard was in the next street, and not in an alehouse. Not that I grudge any man his beer, it would be against my trade."

"With such an evil face, it astonished me that Master Penny listened to the woman, yet he had taken his purse out to give her a groat."

"The gentleman lives in the country, and we have known Noll and his like since we were babes. That is another reason why he is offering you a place in his household; if he sends you to London with a load of timber, you are less likely to be cozened by a fair-speaking false clerk."

"It used to be a tranquil, leafy lane."

"Whatever it was, if you had not happened to be passing, Noll would have cracked the man's skull and tossed the body into the Thames."

"I like a merry thief, like Hob, who used to show us openly the sixpences he had filched at the ring."

"Hob was a rogue, but not a thief. He simply wasn't born to be a stay-at-home. Once he had got enough pieces together to buy himself a buff jerkin, he was off to the wars."

"And there got himself killed or hanged, for he never came home," I said bitterly. I had liked Hob.

"Dost remember how he sprang into the ring with just his stick and a little dagger, and drove the bear out alone, all because a gallant had wagered him that such a feat was impossible? He made me laugh like a fool, and yet I trembled for him."

"And then he was found next morning without a sixpence in his pouch, because he had invited all our beggars to a banquet."

"That was a morning world," Humphries finished his wine slowly sip by sip, "and now, we're at midnight. I am often glad that poor Mr Beaumont died before these changes happened. He was such a sweet, gay gentleman."

I nodded. It was not merely Southwark but the theatres, the very style of playing, that had altered. History and emperors were out of fashion. We had a new hero, the spendthrift rascal who won the rich alderman's daughter. What we had lost when we had left the open air for candlelight! I knew, I had suffered.

"Master Sands, be advised. When I knew you first, you were little taller than a lute string, though much, much broader. Sooner or later the Puritans will have their way, and the theatres will be closed."

"As they tell us. 'I have been bred to my craft since babyhood!' It is a hard choice to make."

"Rather make it yourself than have the world make it for you. It is not every merchant who would take a player into his house."

If only I could know, I thought, staring at the grain of the wood in the table below me. It ran so easily from side to side of the board, with the occasional curve that almost made a leaf, or the currant-shaped stain where a wine drop had fallen. It was so simple, so direct, and nothing about me was either. I owed a duty both to my belly and to my art, and which, I wondered, was the more important? "I shall bring no laurels to Master Awsten's memory now," I said, "whatever may befall me."

"Who knows what you might have brought, if either of your masters had lived. Every pupil has his rights, and it was shameful that none of their fellows looked to you."

"Yes," I agreed, and I looked helplessly at the fire again. How impossible it was to choose a particular moment and say, here because I lifted, or did not lift my cap, my fellowship disowned me. I suppose, after Master Sly was dead, I had trusted too much to Mr Beaumont. I had walked about with my head in the clouds, if he had merely wished me good morrow. Dicky could have told me to my face that he was trying to steal my membership, and I should never have believed him. "I was a boy without a master for two years," I said, "but I was not disobedient, I thought they loved me."

"They said you were proud," Humphries stood up, and raked the sticks into a cascade of sparks, "but who is not, at seventeen? I remember when I was that age, sliding down a roof to drink watered beer with a journeyman, and he fleeced me of a silver sixpence afterwards. I could have had a tankard of home-brewed ale at home for the asking, but it wouldn't have been stolen fruit, and so I risked my life on those tiles."

"Proud! I knew that I was there to serve them, except once, when Mr Beaumont read some verses I had scribbled. It was more like being asleep."

"Even Sly complained that you were always at some gallant's heels, but then it's natural for a boy to follow a proper-looking man."

"That wasn't why I watched them!" I looked up at Humphries, but he was busy, counting the billets that still remained on the hearth. I had envied the courtiers their shirts, not because of the fineness of the linen, but because they were clean. I had always longed to get away from the stench and the flies. "It's true that I hoped at one time, Mr Beaumont would take me to the country. He had told me I could be his page."

"And you not a gentleman's son!"

"As if that mattered nowadays; look at Cotton!" and we both laughed. Cotton's father had been little better than a pedlar, but through some mixture of cunning and false good nature, the son now owned a shop in the neighbourhood of Cheapside.

"I always said that that man was a magician," Humphries ran his thumb round the glass, to collect a stray wine drop, "he built his fortunes on an invisible load of cambric. First he sold it to a young heir, at the end of a drinking party, and then, once the fool was thirsty again, Cotton resells it, for a commission naturally, to an even greater idiot. As far as I am aware, nobody even saw the outside of a bale! And now, what about yourself?" The innkeeper looked me directly in the eyes. "Do you remember protesting to me that if you only had five gold angels in your hand you would leave these 'stinking alleys' and go back to the country?"

"That was long ago, and now this is home." I jerked my head towards the window, because although I could not see through the heavy curtains, I knew that the Thames was on my right and the marshes on my left, and that the few people who were still kind to me lived in the streets between them.

"Faith! boy, can't you ride to visit us on holidays? There are enough of them in the year, or I should not earn sufficient to buy sand for this floor. Mind you bring me up some apples when you come. It must be twenty years since I tasted a Bitter Sweeting; our fruit is bigger nowadays, but it's sour."

"I promise you a sack at Michaelmas." There was no way of making Humphries understand my reluctance to accept the merchant's offer. "Awsten's smile, three good meals a day," the words had revolved in my head for a week, like a ballad I had sung too often, and I wanted these warm, drowsy moments to last, my decision could wait until morning. The rain thundered on the roof, falling heavily and coldly, with an occasional wilder shower threshing through its regular beat. *"Time goes on, Time never turns, Time goes on, and all men with it."* The storm hammered on the tiles, as if it were here only to slam such a phrase into our ears, and I thought suddenly of Westminster, and Sir Walter, with this tempest abroad, preparing through the night for his last voyage.

One Sunday afternoon my father had nodded goodbye to me at his door. I had gone off whistling down the lane, wondering why holidays ever ended. Two days later he was dead of the plague, before a messenger could reach me to tell me that he was ill. When fate flung us about so haphazardly, was either vice or virtue of importance? What difference was there between us and the walnut leaves that this wind was stripping from the neighbouring gardens? Then Fire, the exalted humour, shook me till I seemed to play the wag with Time, and stand outside it. There was wisdom for those who wanted it, though the search was as elusive as for a new road to India. Thinking of this brought Martin to my mind; what had happened to him, was he dead, or had he found his island? I was still dreaming about him when a fist banged on the door, and Humphries got up to let in not only two journeymen come for their beer, but a cold air that whipped my damp collar with a tongue of ice.

The innkeeper served the men, and then came back to our table. "What is there to forgo," he continued irritably, "except the chance to strut in satin for an hour or two, on an empty belly, harder to fill every season."

"I know," I said, "listen to the terrible, sad ballad of Dicky Robinson." I could even smile about the story today.

"I warned you to be careful of that boy, and you were so angry that you would not speak to me for a twelve-month."

"When Dicky came to us, I suppose I compared him with myself. I thought he would be frightened and lonely, and I spent the only coin I had, to buy him some gingerbread. But I verily believe that he knew more before he was breeched than I know now. Besides, he was older, the company had bought him from another player, he must have been fourteen."

"Dicky, frightened! Why, Sands, you were as night and day!"

"I see that now. Yet, remember, we all adored him. Whatever was happening inside that curly head of his, he looked, at will, the modest gentlewoman or the pert, little page. Oh, he was merry; why, I've seen him turn a somersault and wink at the old woman who was mending his cloak, till she had to drop it for laughing. Then he would go off, as grave as you please, and flip a Latin tag that he did not understand, at some fellow newly come to us with a half-written play. If Dicky forgot his lines, he got a reproof, where I should have got a clout. No, he had his will from the beginning. Whatever I had done would have been useless."

"You were in love with him."

"No," I shook my head, "that wasn't love."

"Go to, Sands, it was your age; you were backward then, and not ripe for a girl."

"I loved Mistress Ursula, but she was above my degree. No, Dicky was, as I see it now, the other side of myself."

"Then it is a pity that you did not reverse your places in time. The trouble with you is that you never cared enough about ambition."

"I wanted fame, but that was different." I could never make Humphries understand that my laurel was a word of praise from Mr Beaumont, and so, to break the conversation, I lifted up my wine and drank to him.

"It was all a trick."

"Yes." It was only today with this grave decision in front of me, to leave my craft and become Master Penny's man, that I saw the plot from beginning to end. I even had to smile. It was the stock scene from the new comedy with the cunning maid tripping up the dull-witted son of the house. After Master Sly had died, all the company, and not simply my master, had begun to use me for errands because, they said, I was less likely than my fellows to be found sleeping in an alehouse with the reckoning unpaid. They had flattered me too: "Ask Sands, the little wag has a way with him, he'll get it for you"; and so, instead of studying my notes, or my fence, I had trotted all over Southwark, and half London, with a letter for a girl, or a device to persuade the mercer (whom Gilborne had not paid for two seasons) to let him have some flame-coloured taffeta for the next pastoral. It was much gayer to stand in the crowd and watch the Venetian Ambassador, in silver lace, ride with his train to Windsor than to learn a dull speech about some Roman matron's virtue. Only it was not surprising, when I was absent so often, that Dicky began to slip into parts that I ought to have played. Even tonight I could not decide whether the fellowship were to blame or not. They had played with me at their will, but my real enemy had been my innocent self. "Dicky seemed to like me," I went on, for Humphries, I knew, disliked the boy for the wrong reasons. "Over and over, unless I were playing opposite him, he would pout and refuse to learn his lines. It was difficult for the company, I looked clumsy in petticoats earlier than most boys, and was still too sturdy and childlike for a gallant. Dicky could do anything with that body of his from the day that he joined us. He could flick his hand to his face, and there was a waiting woman on Horseshoe Steps, shrieking in front of you, 'Mercy, rogue, thou hast splashed my petticoat with thy great oars, and I'll be forsworn if the velvet did not cost me a gold piece at Master Lambton's'; then next day, he would win a bout from our fencing master with a trick he had learned, nobody knew how. There wasn't a part he could not play...."

"He was a great actor, I agree."

"His movements came from inside him, and I could only repeat what I was taught. I remember they used to laugh, 'Sands, thou goest through a play as if thou wert walking in thy sleep,' but try as I would, I could not understand the citizens as Dicky could, he turned them inside out."

"That is why you would be better off with Master Penny; you never had your heart in acting, Sands, except once."

"Yet sometimes it was as if something entered into me from the air, and Gilborne would clap my head and say, 'He is waking up,' but it never lasted."

"You changed masters too often."

"They said I was apprenticed to Master Sloth, but I tried, I worked harder than Dicky ever worked in his life, yet some humour failed in me, I was moist and cold."

"You were stunned, boy," Master Humphries said kindly, as if I were sixteen instead of twenty-six. "Sly died before you had got over your first loss, and then Mr Beaumont left you suddenly, for the country."

"They trusted me. They sent me to Aldermanbury with a pouch full of ryals and portugales. I was frightened out of my life that I should be robbed. If they gave me their money to carry, wasn't it natural to assume that when the moment came they would admit me to the company? I suppose I grew careless too, watching Dicky, there were so many things that he could do without a scolding."

"And I thought you an intelligent lad!"

"One day Dicky asked me to take a message to Mistress Barton. He said he wanted to borrow her nephew's cloak for a part. I never suspected that he was courting a girl, and the cloak was verily a cloak for him, the sign that he would be waiting by the orchard gate on the following Sunday. Somebody must have overheard us, because when I got back to the theatre I was given a beating for wasting time in idle gossip. Dicky laughed and told me to take no notice, but I felt that it was unjust, after they had sent me themselves on similar errands, besides I was in a rage over being struck; after all I was almost a man, and so I sulked and did as little as possible during the week. Then one day Master Taylor called me up before him, 'Sands,' he said, 'thou hast been with us ten years, hast thou thought about thy future?' I stood there like a fool, twiddling my cap. The company had been my school since before my father died, and it had never entered my silly head that they could dismiss me from their fellowship. 'Why, no,' I stammered, and wondered if there were to be changes. Sometimes an actor came to us from one of the other companies.

"Master Taylor looked at me for a moment, and I know now that he was uneasy, because he kept twisting and untwisting a bit of ribbon. 'How long is it since you last played Euphrasia?' he asked, and in my stupid confidence, I smiled and answered, 'They say I look too old to play the woman.'

"There was a dirty tassel lying on the floor that had been torn off a banner. I was wondering how long it had been lying on the ground, when Master Taylor continued, 'We think, Sands, that it will be in thine own interest if we part company for a while. The other boys are younger, and thou are frequently a poor example to them.' He did not mention Dicky by name, but I knew whom he meant. 'I have always done my duty,' I said stiffly, because I had restrained Dicky from a dozen escapades. 'Have you?' he said, and smiled. I could only look guilty because though it was harmless enough, Dicky and I had been rambling up the river the previous day, dreaming about what we would do when we were men, and, forgetting the hour, had come home late for supper.

"'Thou hast a right to get thy bread from the craft to which thou wert bound,' Master Taylor continued, though

I was so dazed that I hardly heard him. 'The Queen's Company are short of a man, and as we do not wish to stand in the way of thy advancement we have recommended thee to Master Beeston.' He spoke as if this were a great gift, but it was sending me to the ranks after I had borne the colours. Whenever has a hired man in a poor fellowship risen to be a master? I was too proud to defend myself, if this were to be the thanks for my faithful service, so I bowed and asked, 'At what hour shall I present myself to Master Beeston?'

"Master Taylor looked startled then, and even sorrowful. Doubtless he had expected me to cry for mercy, or swear that I'd have the law on them. 'Go to the Bull tomorrow at two of the afternoon, and say that you come with our blessing.' (It was you instead of thou, I noticed; so I was become a stranger already.) 'Perhaps you can come back to us after you have had a few more years of experience,' he added, and so honestly that you might have supposed that he meant it; but players are used to dissembling. If they had offered me Burbage's own parts, I would never have returned to them. I had not deserved to be cast away like the broken tassel at my feet."

"Six shillings a week," Humphries looked down cruelly at my broken boots, "with half a share you would have had at least fifteen shillings."

"Or they could have kept me with the company in the smaller parts as they did a couple of my fellows, but they were angry, I never knew why, at my friendship with Dicky."

"And what did Dicky say?" the innkeeper asked.

"He cried, he spoke of Castor and Pollux, and swore that they were separating us because some fool was jealous. He even spoke to Mr Taylor, and got a clout on the head for his pains."

"Did you see him speak to Taylor?"

"No, I was getting my clothes together, when he came up to my room, sobbing that now I was a man I should get another friend. I was so busy consoling him that I forgot my own fortunes."

"Dissembling brat!" Humphries snorted.

"I believe he meant it — at the time. Whatever he said was real to him, only there was so much power behind the words, they could not last."

"And too much air in you, Sands; what you needed was some good common earth and anger."

"I knew that Dicky liked me. I had got him out of a dozen pranks."

"A gull! A gull among gulls!" Humphries leaned back against the wall, his shoulders heaving with laughter, though his eyes were kind. "If I didn't know that you had all your wits about you now, I should say that you were ripe for Bedlam. No, boy, you had no one to protect you, and you blundered into their trap like a trusting innocent. The company wanted to keep a membership open, whether your Dicky knew about it or not, because once he was grown every company in London would be after him. He was a much better actor."

"I never wanted to take chances from Dicky, I admired him too much." Even after all these years, I could hear him asking, as if from the other side of this rain, "Sands, where art thou, is my ruff straight?" And the simple words were lovelier than a madrigal.

"Verily, Humphries," I continued, with the memories crowding through my brain, "he came once through the curtains of the tiring room, after the saddest death of an innocent maid that a louse-ridden poet ever penned. All of us, and we were his fellow players, had our eyes full of tears. And what does he do? Whilst the crowd is clapping, and even the gallants are stamping their stools on the boards, he snatches one of Mother Goslin's pies out of a fold of his gown, and bites it in half! Then he thrusts the one bit into my mouth, and the other piece into his own, and totters back like a white ghost to make his legge, very modestly, with his jaw full of plums."

"He was a mad and merry wag, I grant you, but did he never help you, Sands, afterwards?"

"If he did not, I was the one to blame. We worked on week days, and when we had our liberty, on Sunday evenings, Dicky always had a dozen invitations. Didst hear of the time when he went in a farthingale to a banquet, and nobody suspected that he was not a country maid! They laughed about it in the taverns for a month." I did not want to confess this to Humphries, but I had also been ashamed of my clothes. The last time that I had walked with Dicky across Tower Bridge, he had looked liked a Gentleman of the Bedchamber in the carnation and silver suit that some admirer had given him, and I had seemed his serving man in my short, old-fashioned cloak.

"All the same, you had been their good and loyal boy, and they ought to have found a place for you, not have turned you off to Mr Beeston."

"At least I have seen half England," I answered, shrugging my shoulders. The only brave thing about the Queen's Players was the name. They were always in trouble or debt, and for a time I had joined their second company in the provinces. "We might have been soldiers," I added lightly, "for we slept on hay in bat-ridden barns, and once on dirty boards above a pig sty. I remember one week we had a pitched battle with the sheriff's men, because a Puritan had complained that our warrant was out of order, and in the very next town a crazy knight invited us all to a banquet. It was a mad life, and whenever I got back to Southwark my clothes were as full of patches as the plays we had acted, but I suppose it was a healthy one. None of us took the plague, and I missed the riots last Shrove Tuesday when they burst into Mr Beeston's house and burned the play books and apparel."

"So, so, when I was a boy," Humphries drew his stool a

little nearer to the fire, "the theatres had something for all of us, cobblers or courtiers. Now your masques are too fantastical for a plain man, and as for the Bull, I never thought to agree with a Puritan, but it ought to be closed. It is fuller of lewd songs than thieves."

I nodded, there was much truth in the innkeeper's complaint, although if we had changed, so had all England. "Still, they sometimes listen to the old tragedies in the country," I said, "I met a carter once who spoke me Tamerlane's speech without missing a word, and he had only heard it once."

"You can keep your travel," Humphries grunted, "tell me what a man gains from it? Look where poor Sir Walter is tonight! If he had contented himself with studying his books in the Tower, instead of rushing off on a fool's errand to Guiana, he would be playing a game of tables with his wife, with a calm old age in front of him."

"He dreamed of freedom for thirteen years. Besides, he wanted land for people like Hob. It is better to fight the wilderness than be hanged for stealing sheep."

"Maybe, maybe, but the trouble goes deeper than mere land. If they had left the commons alone, so that a man could pasture his beast as he has done since the beginning of time, we should not need these wild Virginia ventures; what do they ever bring us but monsters?"

Some people argued that the new method of farming was giving us more food, because the hedges were a wind break

and kept stray beasts from trampling the crops, but I did not
want to discuss this tonight, I only wanted to be warm. The
wind blew more and more violently, and I remembered that
when the maid had swept the summer rushes from my room,
to burn them, with other trash, on a neighbour's bonfire, she
had forgotten to bring up the fresh bundle, so that my attic
would be bitterly cold. I stared at the hearth, and wished that
I could sleep here until April. Humphries was drowsy too;
perhaps he was dreaming about the time when there had been
two country girls chattering in the kitchen, and a drawer, always in a fresh white apron, to help him with the ale. How
long was it since his wife had died? Two years, no, it must be
almost three. I had been at Norwich with the company that
summer, and had only heard of it on my return. I was glad
that she had been spared seeing the decay of our fortunes.
If a maid had brought me a trencher of her famous bacon
pie tonight, I could not have paid for it. What had formerly
been worth a penny, now cost sixpence. I smoothed out my
collar and prepared to leave, because it was getting late, but
Humphries roused himself and pulled me back. "We must
drink a parting glass," he protested, and when I would have
argued, shook his head; "a night like this, the least I can offer
an old friend is a little sack. It's good of its kind, even if it is
not the Burgundy that I used to serve to Master Sly."

"Sometimes I think that the inconstancy is in the Crown
itself," I murmured, but Humphries was so nearly asleep that

he did not hear the treasonable words. "Once a ruler dies, the virtues of yesterday become the vices of today. Look at Queen Elizabeth! Her symbol was courage. King James wants peace, even as they say now, with dishonour. Men go up, men go down, like the painted wheel of Fortune that they show us at the fairs." A snore answered me, then Humphries stirred, rubbed his eyes, and poured himself out more wine.

"Look, sir," I continued, although I knew that he was too sleepy to listen, "long before I set eyes on Master Awsten, when I was still so tiny that I could not manage the two steps between our kitchen and the yard, there was an old stableman who used to tell me stories. They were chiefly about his horses or a fat, grey pigeon he had tamed, but sometimes as it grew dark, he would take me on his knee and start, very slowly, *'The bell began to toll in St Mary's Tower.'* This made me shiver delightfully, because I thought then that Plague was the name of a dragon. My mother was so terribly afraid of it, and talked so much about its poisonous breath. *'The carpenters put down their saws, the tanners hung up their skins, and the prentices came with staves, then we all marched together to Tilbury.'* I did not know where Tilbury was, because I was so young that I had hardly been out of my own street, but it had a long, distant sound about it like the end of the world. *'We sent the little boys,'* and here he paused, and looked at me gravely, *'to feed the horses.'* 'But how could they feed them?' I used to ask, for this bit puzzled me, 'unless you lift me up, I cannot even reach Dobbin his carrot.' I can see him now (it was a much clearer picture than any these flames could make) answering me solemnly, *'Babes grow quickly in times of trouble.'* For weeks afterwards I used to feel my head every morning, wondering how much I had grown along the pillow in the night. *'It grew darker and darker,'* with these words he started to rock me slowly on his knee, *'the bells were silent, but the old watchman of St Mary's Church began to climb up the tower. It took him a long time to reach the top, because his knees were trembling, and his mind was full of the great danger that hung over our City. At last he could see the river below, moving just as sleepily as a little boy whose bedtime had come round again, and he wondered what would happen if it were not called Thames any more, but had a Spanish name? Then suddenly, so far away that he thought at first it was a star, there came a light. Presently something blazed beyond Lambeth Marshes — there was a third flame — a fourth — as many fires on all the hills as there were people left in London. The bells began to ring again, very merrily, the little ones like morris bells, and the big ones that sound like water. There was rejoicing such as England had never seen, nor ever will again, for by God's grace the Spanish Fleet was broken, and her Majesty and all her realm were safe.'* With these words he would swing me triumphantly up to his shoulder, and then take me home to my supper."

Yes, in spite of this rain thundering on the flooded street,

I could still smell the dusty, late summer grasses and the stableman was nearer to me than Dicky's face or my own fortunes. "Ralegh is almost the last survivor of '88. Are we going to sit here, and do nothing to save him?"

I must have spoken too loudly, because one of the journeymen looked up. "Have a care, Master Sands, those are bitter words, and they say that the knight plotted against the King, although I agree, for my part, that he deserves a better fate."

"Sands meant no harm," Humphries interposed hastily, "he is only sad that so old a gentleman should die for a foreign king's pleasure."

There was such a violent knocking outside that we all looked up, half expecting to see a constable enter and rebuke us, but it was only two other wayfarers in search of shelter. A gust of wind almost blew the glasses from the board, and Humphries had to put his shoulder to the great door before he could close it behind them. They flung their wet cloaks to Bess, sat down at the vacant table, and stared contemptuously about them. "A sorry country inn," the younger man muttered, but loud enough for us to hear him. "Some claret wine," he commanded harshly, "if you have any fit to be drunk."

Humphries made no reply, but my neighbour, a powerful fellow from the tannery by the river, looked up angrily from his ale. "If the gentlemen find our Southwark cheer too humble for them," he growled, "we are not a mile from London Bridge, and it is a cool, pleasant evening for a walk."

"Nay, we meant no harm," the older of the two answered hastily, "we have ridden up from Kent to see the Procession of the Barges tomorrow, but the gale was so fierce that we left our horses at the *Angel,* and meant to walk to a friend of mine who is expecting us for supper. With all this sleet, you cannot see a hand in front of you, and we must have taken a wrong turning among your winding lanes. All we want is some wine to warm us before we go on our way."

"It will be a brave sight if the wind falls," the other journeyman said hopefully. He was an inquisitive little fellow who worked for a tailor, and never missed a pageant if he could help it. "The Lord Mayor's barge is to be hung with cloth of silver, only you will have to be up early to get a place along the bank."

"Wind or no wind," the tanner grunted, "there will be plenty of space tomorrow. All the citizens will be at Westminster. What is a rag of silk compared with the pitiful end of so gallant and worthy a knight?"

"Gallant and worthy," the rougher of our visitors sneered. "Why, Ralegh thought of nothing but his own glory."

"No," I interrupted, surprised at my own temerity, "he thought of the Queen"; whether it were of the Cynthia he served or of his own Bess made no matter.

"You player fellows see everything as bombast," he looked me insolently up and down, "or I would thrash you for uttering such base, seditious words. The King's fault is clemency.

Ralegh should have lost his head at the end of his trial, fifteen years ago. It was plain to all that he had been conspiring, not only against his Sovereign but the realm."

I sprang up, but Master Humphries stepped forward between us. "Peace, gentlemen, I want no quarrelling in my house. Leave matters of state to the men whom they concern, and let us keep to our own affairs." He dragged his stool round, so that he now had his back to me, and added, "I hear you had a good nut harvest in Kent this year; if the old saying is true, that means a hard winter."

The man nodded, but refused to be drawn into any conversation. We sat, listening to the rain on the roof, without speaking a word. I wondered uneasily if the men were informers; it was an old trick to go from tavern to tavern and provoke a quarrel, so that the innkeeper would bribe them to be rid of them, because a complaint about disorder to a justice meant a fine or a bribe or both. Their story about the ride from Kent was a lie. No countryman would have recognised me as a player, and I wondered in a numb and ever growing fear, what they wanted in this poor, desolate inn? Humphries, I saw, was as anxious as myself. The tanner drained his ale, got up, and left without the customary greeting. The man who had threatened me looked round our bare but clean room as contemptuously as if it had been a hovel. Suddenly, to our relief, his companion pulled out a silver coin, and said, "I think the wind is dropping a little;

if you have a boy who can guide us through this maze of gardens, we will return to the *Angel* for the night."

"I will get a lantern at once." Humphries lost no time in going towards the kitchen, calling for the old ostler as he went. I followed him to get my cloak. "Shall I wait?" I whispered, once we were out of earshot. "Those men came for no lawful purpose."

Humphries shook his head. "I would sooner you were away before they leave. They had some villainy in mind that the storm prevented, but they like me as little as I like them, and there are too many people in the inn for them to risk anything here." He set the lantern on the table with a clatter and added, in a loud voice, as though he were afraid that our visitors might accuse us of conspiracy, "You are right, good sir, you are right, bed is the best place for us all on a night like this." Then he unbolted the side door, and I gasped for breath as I met the wind. It blew everything away, memory, the warmth of our conversation and the wine; I felt that it would rip my jerkin from my ribs, and by the time that I had walked the few yards to Mother Crofton's gate, no otter hound, back from a day's hunting in a muddy stream, could have been wetter, or more eager for shelter.

The dirty boards at the side of my bed were thick with dust. The servant had taken the used rushes away, but had not swept the floor. I hated to complain because Mother

Crofton was growing old, but I remembered my boyhood, when the boards had been so clean that we could have spread our food on them, and the flagstones in the yard had been fresh and scrubbed. Now with her swollen, gouty legs, Mother Crofton could hardly struggle up the winding stairs after a pert girl who would not empty a pitcher if she could avoid it. There were still the same number of lodgers in the house, but our sixpences bought less of everything each year. Brooms had doubled in price, there was a dearth of scouring sand, and when a carpenter had been fetched to mend a warped door, he had charged more for an hour's work than old Hodge had charged for a day. Life was always going to get better when Easter was over or the plague had ceased; instead, it grew steadily worse.

The wind seemed to come through the walls, thick as they were, but the atmosphere in the small attic remained stale and damp. I had left as many clothes as possible to dry by the kitchen fire, but my once good coverlet had worn thin, and though I had piled all the garments I could find on top of me, I was still too cold to sleep.

I turned over, thinking of the willows where I had first met Mr Beaumont. How they would sway tonight, with their tips almost touching the water, as I was tossing here, swaying up and down, unable to decide my future. Ought I to be faithful to my craft? Ought I to leave London? Was it truly a choice between body and spirit? "Oh, Mr Francis,"

I murmured aloud (as if saying the words could give any comfort!), "here is Destiny holding out her hands, but they are closed; as you once said, nothing is simple; is there no third way, what would you have me do?" Naturally there was no answer, a tile clattered down from the roof into the road, it seemed colder and the half-light was gloomier than complete darkness. Ought I to acknowledge that the company faced fresh difficulties every season, and turn to a new master? Ought I to remain with my fellows and starve? Ought I, ought I not? I thought of the willows sixty miles away in Kent, and groaned.

I could understand Humphries' anger. "What is the merchant asking you to relinquish?" he had said in surprise, after he had given me the message, and I had not hurried at once to Master Penny's inn. "Aren't you tired of playing the gentleman? A good linsey is better than a nobleman's discarded carnation." Yet this was more than moving from Southwark to the country, it was a change in degree. A good servant was bound to respect his master's wishes, and if I had to echo opinions contrary to my own, month after month, how long would it be before through sheer repetition I believed them, and lost my independence? Perhaps Mr Beaumont would have approved the change; he might have said, "This uncertain, almost soldier's life is not for you, Sands, take the body and leave the soul, go back to a narrow duty and three good meals a day." Then

I seemed to hear that gruff, commanding voice answering, "You are all stubborn serge, boy, with an extraordinary slash of color taken from a bird's nest of fantasy somewhere in the homespun. Hasn't the wind-blown been more to you than the wool? To forget the Muses is to forget learning, it will be hard to begin your letters again at the criss-cross row, after the primer was halfway ended." Oh, what was I to do? Surely it was better to serve the merchant than to beg? Fewer and fewer people came to see us play, we were out of fashion, dusty, and at war with one another, and it was two weeks since I had had any wages.

They said that Mr Beaumont had been moon-struck at his death. He had gone back to Kent long before I had been dismissed from the company, but Dicky had met me once on a hot afternoon and had invited me to drink with him at a small inn, much frequented by players. I remember that we had both sat there wondering what to say, a few months had made us such strangers to one another. I was thinking of some excuse to leave, when a gentleman had entered, muffled in a cloak, almost as if he were afraid of daylight. "Look, James," Dicky had whispered mockingly, "here comes the Knight of the Burning Taper himself." To our dismay, as the figure came nearer to us, I had recognised Mr Beaumont. He had stopped in front of our table, but without greeting us; instead he had enquired in a soft, strange voice of almost unnatural beauty, "Suppose, my puppets, this my play were the real world, and all else mere dissembling, would you walk through it so faint-heartedly?" I had felt him looking directly at my face. "Mr Beaumont," I had begun, but he had stared as if he had never seen me, and had added reproachfully, "Words are numbers, and you turn them into brute sounds, hast never heard of Pythagoras?" Then his friend, Fletcher, had taken him gently by the arm and had led him away, and old Armin, who was himself to die so soon afterwards, had muttered compassionately, "Poor rascal, he has slept out in the moonlight, and now Selena claims him for her own."

I had never seen Mr Beaumont again. He had gone back to Sundbridge, we had heard that he was ill, a year later we had followed his coffin to the Abbey. I had thought of trying to find some wild daffodils for a wreath, but, was it laziness or sorrow, it had seemed foolishness to bring flowers to him. I had seen Mistress Ursula among the mourners; she had looked old, and my heart had not leapt any longer when she passed us, going down the aisle between two of his kinsmen. I had had only a strange sensation that I could put my fist through the wooden pew. My own part had rung in my ears, Bellario's words (and how many years was it since I had said them?):

> "It is but giving over of a game
> That must be lost."

He had written his own epitaph. This was a harsh world. I could not be sorry that his too visionary heart had peace from it.

And afterwards?

It was Ralegh who had tried to seek the answer. Once during that enchanted summer, when I had taken a cloak to Mistress Ursula on the terrace, she had said, "They are talking about the Captain, but Guiana does not content him. He wants to explore heaven, yes, and to chart it too." I had been thinking at that moment that I would rather be the rose that was pinned to her kirtle than younger brother to Mr Francis, and I could still remember the prick of my jealousy that she was listening to such talk, when she had added sorrowfully, and as if she were fond of him, "Surely fear must wake him in the night, he soars so high."

Ah well, it was one thing to leap with the full powers of the mind, and the sword arm at its greatest strength, towards combat and controversy, and another to wait in the Guard House at Westminster, in the chill of age, with the minutes revolving slowly and swiftly at one and the same time. If Ralegh died, something of England's freedom would perish as well, at the command of a foreign king, and to protect our corrupt and dicing courtiers from any alarm of possible war. Would nobody try to save him, I wondered; oh, if only Prince Henry, who so loved him, were alive! And what do you intend to do yourself, Master Sands (one side of my brain murmured), are you going to stand there with tears in your eyes, to watch the execution? Call on the crowd to follow you, shout for a rescue? But suppose the guards should seize me before I had time to draw my dagger (here came another whisper) and I were flung on to the dirty floor of a fever-ridden gaol until the pestilence rotted my guts? Nobody would know or care where I was. Courage, we needed courage, but this was just the virtue that, in this freezing moment of the night, I did not have.

A shutter clattered somewhere, and I jumped. Was it the intruders from the *Plough* battering at the door? It was not the weather that had driven those bullies into the inn; they had been looking for someone, and had known who I was. I leapt up, looked to the latch, but the staircase was empty, it was merely the ruffling wind loosening more tiles from the roof. I could feel my heart thumping, as I went over the previous week; had I said anything that could be remotely considered treasonable? I knew that I was innocent, all Southwark echoed with the same resentment, there was little love in London for Spain. Then suddenly, and I sat down in terror on my pallet, I knew who the men were. Thieves had a captain to whom they took their loot; the fellows were Noll's friends, come to avenge him. Unless I wished a dagger in my back, I must contrive to get away to the country on the morrow. I leaned over and picked up the blanket, I even pulled it over my ears, as if a strip of thin cloth could keep out the evil of this night! Mice scuffled along the old timber, and as I listened, waiting for the morning, the gale rattled, answering them, "King or journeyman, pilgrim or poet, my lady earth will be nurse to you at the end."

It was early and cold, different from that Trinidad sun whence Ralegh had so lately sailed. He would have a freezing walk to the block. Perhaps it was only the weather that had brought people out in their everyday clothes, but there was no colour, not a ribbon nor rosette to mark the Lord Mayor's day; we tramped, as if to an unwilling muster, with nothing brighter in the dark line of cloaks than a servingman's blue jacket, or an ash-coloured hood. The wind nipped our faces until the women's cheeks were as mottled as a spoiling apple, and there was neither good humour nor friendly shoving as we walked, stopped to let an officer pass, and shuffled on again, without a word, without even looking at our neighbours.

It took me longer than I had expected to cross London Bridge. On the City side, near the landing stage, I looked back at Southwark. The Thames lay between us, grey and battered like an old man's morion; even the outline of the bank had an unfamiliar shape. What had become of all the trees? The elm that I had watched from Master Sly's window had been blown down in a gale, but had they felled three oaks, or four, to make the path to Lambeth Steps? Over there the Globe had burned, and with it all the emperors. The new building was solid and brave, but it was an empty shell, I owed it no allegiance. There were more boats, more houses, and fewer birds. "Way," a fellow shouted, pushing me violently to one side, "what were you doing last night, sluggard? You can't sleep your ale off here." The two women behind him laughed as I jumped, and to get rid of their mockery I turned up the next alley, in the direction of Cheapside.

It was dangerous to loiter among these narrow gutters, but what had I on me worth stealing? On such a day, the thieves could smell a merchant out quicker than a flea could hop from a linsey collar to a velvet mantle. The air stank, and I made what haste I could between the piles of rubbish tossed out to rot on the ground, and the pools of filthy water. I was thankful when I reached the main road again a few minutes later, although the crowd was now so dense that the Guard had difficulty in clearing enough space for a horseman wearing the City colours to pass between us at a walk. I began to wonder if I should reach Westminster in time, but it was impossible to turn, the press held me, I could not move my arms. If half the men had brought a quarterstaff or a bill, we could have overwhelmed the Guard through sheer weight of numbers.

"Don't cry, my dear," a broad Devon voice said just in front of me, "the King will reprieve him at the last moment, just as he did before." They were country people, and the wife had a blue and white kerchief pressed to her eyes. "No," she sobbed, "no, and he is worth all the princes in Christendom."

"Oh, take her home, she has no stomach for a beheading," a fellow jeered, lifting a nosegay to his face so that he might not smell our wet jerkins.

"More stomach than you who cannot haul a rope," she flung at her tormentor, as I pressed forward to stand between them. Her son, no doubt, was a sailor; perhaps from Ralegh's own ship.

"There'll be a reprieve, you'll see," the husband repeated soothingly, "they will lead him to the scaffold just as they did before, and the herald will come on his great, white horse to read out the King's Pleasure."

"And then Sir Walter will kneel, and thank God for His mercy and the King for his clemency," another woman added.

"I'd as soon see him die as kneel," somebody growled, an old fellow this time, in the short cloak that had been all the fashion when I had been a boy.

"Such a fuss about a traitor," Master Nosegay answered, but a dozen voices yelled at him, "Ralegh is no traitor though there are enough in England who are." We might be afraid to speak in the alehouses, but we knew more about the Spanish influence at Court than our rulers wished.

"Silence, silence." The Guard began laying about them with their staves.

"'Tis a judgement on him," a woman murmured, "for sweet Essex his sake."

"Do we know," Greybeard shrugged his shoulders, "do any of us understand?"

"Silence," the Guard shouted again, pressing us back, so as to leave a narrow space down the length of the road.

"They will reprieve him," the countryman repeated for the third time obstinately.

"Who wants to see a singing bird taken back to a dark cage," I quoted, and my neighbour answered, "I would Prince Henry were alive."

"They say the Queen is doing all she can to save him," a carpenter muttered; then he glanced round anxiously to see that no constables were present.

"King James never listens to her, the poor lady," an old gossip answered angrily; then she lifted a cloth from her basket, and added in a loud whisper, with an eye on the Guard, who were by this time further up the road, "Hot cakes, who'll buy my hot cakes?" knowing as well as we did that this was no place to cry her wares.

"It's the Spaniards," a boy began, but another youth slapped him over the mouth.

"He is paying for the Armada," I shouted, "he saved you then, will you do nothing for him now?"

"Save Ralegh, save Ralegh," the cry was going up the line like wind.

"And have war," the man with the nosegay flung at us.

The fickle crowd paused, and I heard the captain of the

Guard threaten us with the Counter. "We don't want war," a fat fellow muttered, scratching a flea bite on his ear, "it would stop the malmsey coming in, and the price of pepper would go up again."

"I remembered my father telling me that the year after the Armada, sugar was a noble a pound."

"It would *not* mean war," I protested, "the Spaniards are bluffing, they would not fight." Hadn't we all seen a bully slink out of a tavern, the moment that the quietest fellow there reached for his sword? Besides, if we abandoned the leader who had served us, our own sacrifices lost their purpose. It opened the door to all that was evil in Man.

"How do you know?" Master Nosegay swept the Armada and its glories away with a flourish of his herbs. "The days of your glass-splintering pirates are over, thank heaven." I felt my fists clench, because I knew that he meant Grenville. "These same Spaniards whom my lord citizens distrust so much," and he looked round him scornfully, "have civilised us a little. What kind of a world was it when clowns left their sheep to ramble the high seas? What were they but common robbers? But I forget, you had a woman over you."

"I would the Queen were over us today," Greybeard answered, and elbowed his way towards us.

"What happened to your roving Englishmen?" The voice behind the posy mocked us lightly; "either they died of fever or came home to beg, with a story about a two-headed baboon, an animal that existed, my friends, only in their drunken fancies."

"I know a younger son who went to Trinidad, and he returned with a leather jack full of gold."

"Stolen from its rightful owners, the Spaniards. They were in the Indies a century before your pirates."

"Ralegh was no pirate. He drew the Indians to him in friendship, and would have made a great, fair empire where they and the English settlers could have lived in fellowship, side by side."

"Then if you love your Ralegh so, rescue him," the fellow taunted. Then, perceiving that we were at fever heat, he ducked skilfully under the raised arm of a pikeman who had come to see what the disturbance was, and disappeared into the crowd.

"Informer," Greybeard muttered, and I nodded, but the people were silent and uneasy, under the eyes of a constable who had placed himself at the end of our line.

"Don't elbow me, you rascal, I was here an hour before you." The shrill, high voice made us all look up. In the flurry, an apprentice had pulled untied a bow of soiled, scarlet ribbon that was dangling from a woman's cloak.

"Calm yourself, mother, you'll see as much as any of us when the time comes."

"Mother! Don't mother me, that was a bride last seven night."

"For the fourth time?" the prentice asked, and the crowd roared.

"I want to go home," a child whimpered; he was sitting on a nurse's shoulder, and I could see that the babe was frightened. "You promised me that we were going to see the barges."

"Quiet," the nurse hushed him firmly, "'tis a very gallant gentleman who is about to die."

"If we all went to the King, and prayed him on our knees...?"

"What do we matter to the King? Except to pay him taxes."

"Give way," the Guard shouted, "give way, do you want the Horse to charge you?" Then a great roar went up from the press in front of us, died down, and we stood wedged together in an unnatural stillness.

"They are bringing him out," Greybeard muttered, clutching at my arm. I saw a white face above the sea of heads, very noble. He lifted his hand. Then pikes came between us, the caps turned, and we felt them move towards the centre of the Yard.

"I was with him at Jarnac," Greybeard whispered. "He came to warm his hands at our fire. He always felt the cold. I remember we thought him a raw, untested lad, for he said so sorrowfully that he pitied any fellow, friend or foe, who had to spend his last night on earth asleep in such mud, but you should have seen him in the battle the next day, he snapped a captain's sword in two, as if the blade had been a straw."

"*Down with Spain, down with Spain.*" West-Country voices mingled with the London ones, yet I knew that though men could bear great sorrow, and sometimes love, they could not suffer gratitude, else we should have burst the ranks and carried him away to safety and to France.

"It was a rich country full of vines, but the Huguenots were sober fellows. They always dressed in grey. He was only a poor gentleman volunteer, but I never saw him without a jewel in his cap."

A voice began to speak. We were too far off to hear the words, although the people became so still that they hardly seemed to breathe. I looked from head to head and beyond the uneven line of shoulders, apprehended the Narrow Seas. *The ships saved us,* I thought, we needed no new, scholastic elegies, it could all be said in the one phrase of four words, and behind the ships there was Her Majesty and a dozen men, and of them all, Ralegh was the only survivor. So Gondomar sat there, behind a curtain, and waited for Spain's revenge. "It was thirty years ago," I whispered, "just thirty years."

Perhaps he was remembering the deer that had come to drink from the silver waters of the Orinoco, or the grave where his son was buried, that rough, gay copy of his father. He might be thinking of the clear dawns in France, or of the swaying ship's ladder of his fortunes? Then I knew that these were my fantasies, at such a moment he would have one memory only, that of the day when he had spread his cloak (and they said that it had been his only one) before his lady. "He loved Elizabeth," I murmured, "because she was Cynthia, not because she was Queen."

Then the caps came off, line by line along the crowd, the prayers had begun. Was he thinking of God, of the great, daring search that had frightened his fellow citizens into calling him an atheist, because he wanted to rise above mortal narrowness into the fire of the spheres? I stood there praying that he might have comfort on his journey, some sense of help towards his chosen harbour. "Let him see the beacons," I kept whispering to myself, "let the beacons guide him." Thirty years. It was longer than his son had lived, a mere moment to such savage foes.

There was a terrible silence.

The people swayed, I could not move my arms, there were hundreds of us, but we were helpless; where was Reason in this bleak disaster? A roar started that was at once a howl and a moan. "God have mercy on him," people whimpered, who had not lifted a hand to save him. "For all they said, he made a good end." The cake woman dabbed her cheeks.

"If this is the reward they give to the captain who fought for us," my Devonshire companion sobbed, "there is no justice on earth."

"Nor honour," the soldier groaned; there were tears in his

eyes. "Your looting rascal is better than your colour bearer, he is not so stupid as to believe in duty."

"There will be no war," a scrivener asserted, but what could such appeasement bring us? We could refuse to face the dragon today. It would return towards us, double-headed, on the morrow. *"Disperse, disperse,"* the Guard were using their staves, *"give way, give way,"* the ominous bell of their far off cries tolled not for a man, but a nation. "The guilt is on us," the soldier said, "this will not lightly be forgiven us." Then he added, in an anguished shout, "The King's enemies betrayed him," and a passer-by answered with a line from the ballad, "Greybeard, *that's no news."*

A cold terror began to creep through my own blood. It was over, the sacrifice had been in vain, morality was a beggar's fire against a rising darkness. I moved with the crowd, aimlessly, shivering under my cloak, not caring where I was going. "I marvel that he did not sail direct to France," a waterman muttered, on my left. "But he knew his story was true. He trusted to the King's honour." The Devon farmer said, in a puzzled voice, "Then he was a fool." A third fellow laughed as he turned to push his way through a tavern door. The great signs above the shops swung over our heads, we tramped drearily along the cobbles until I felt from nowhere a hand touch my arm. I jumped as if the brawlers of the night before, or Death himself were beckoning me, but it was only an old servingman who had been pressed against me by the multitude. "Have a care," I snarled harshly, as if the new corruption had crept already into my veins, "the street is wide enough, there is room in it for all."

As I spoke, my hesitation vanished. Master Penny had waited to see the Procession of the Barges. If I wanted to remain alive, I must reach his inn before he rode away, make some excuse for my tardiness, and accept the service that he had offered me with gratitude. It would be better to smell the Kentish air, and watch another April open in the lanes, than to lie in an alley with a dagger between my shoulders. My heart thumped, I pushed to left and right until I was out of the crowd, then I turned into Cripplegate and almost ran towards his lodging.

V

"But giving over of a game."

1626.

T WAS TOO HOT FOR OCTOBER; it might still be late August. The light caught the curved rosettes on the oak chest that stood against the wall, and there was the unfamiliar feeling of a carpet under my feet. If it had not been for an old woman crying marjoram...marjoram...in the street outside, I could well have been sitting in some Italian palace. "I cannot offer you more, Sands," Mr Sutton said quietly, "last year we paid you five pieces a load." Like most merchants now, he had given up the old-fashioned fur-trimmed robe, and as I looked up at his sharp, white face above the magnificent lace collar, I was reminded of a councillor presiding at some assembly of state.

"Our costs have risen so much," I protested, "bread has doubled in price during the last few years, and consequently wages are higher. Then there is the monopoly on rope…" Everybody complained, yet Sutton's high-backed chair must have cost him three times more than he was willing to offer for the best timber in Kent.

"Agreed, agreed," Sutton leaned forward and put his finger tips together as if considering some legal point, "you hear the same story wherever you dine. This country is being ruined for a shot taffety cloak. A handsome fellow has only to caper into a masque, the King nods, and we have another monopoly on our shoulders. What did I tell you last year, when the populace was shouting that new brooms sweep clean? I said that nothing would change, that the courtiers would sway the young King as easily as the old, and that prices would go up again. When my grandmother bought a bolt of cloth, it lasted her for twenty years. I had to get a mantle for my Lord Mayor's banquet, and if a drop of water touches it, the colour spreads to the hem. The dyes are bad, the wool is rotten, and we have to pay good silver to some nameless gull who has caught the King's ear, for permission to buy such miserable wares. It's enough to send an honest man to Virginia."

I wanted to gain time and nodded, though I could not see the worthy Sutton risking the discomforts of such a voyage. "Surely your arras is new? It is finer than anything they have at Whitehall."

"Whitehall!" Sutton smiled condescendingly, as if I were

a yokel open-mouthed before a painted board. "How can you compare my poor dwelling with a palace! Still, it is a good piece in its way, and I would it were my own. It's a pledge I had from a gentleman who sailed to Ragusa. I took some small share in his venture, and he left it with me against the day of his return."

"You have no need of a garden, sir, with such a panel in front of you." I got up to examine it more closely; actually it was a little florid for my taste, with apples and leaves wound most curiously about a nymph. "Is it Italian?" I asked.

"No, French." I could see that my admiration pleased him. "Only last night I was saying to my wife, 'See that your maids keep the tapestry free from dust, this is the season for the ships to arrive. The owner may return and claim it.' The little rogue importuned me most prettily to buy her one in its place. She protests that she can never dine again in front of bare boards."

"Perhaps the gentleman will not come back. When I think of the gales we had this September, I marvel any vessels can survive their fury. Besides," I added uneasily, "there was a ship taken by pirates, not two hours' sail out of Dover."

"As near as that," Sutton looked at me with more interest, "what do they say about it in your part of the country?"

"They grumble. They complain that there are no captains left, that they pay good silver towards a fleet, but it is never there when it is wanted, and that food that used to cost a groat now costs sixpence."

"Agreed, agreed. Without meat a knave cannot keep his flock, and without wool how is a merchant to live, and without your merchants for a King to borrow from, what would happen to this discontented City? Still, the lure of silver lace remains. If a man ventures to the East and back but once, he may make his fortune from a single cargo."

"For my master's sake, I hope your voyages are successful; then you will be able to offer him a fair price for his timber."

"Come, Sands, five pieces is fair value; dost think I do not know how many my friend Abbott paid for his quarter boards?"

"And did you see the wood? It was green, knotted stuff that no carpenter would touch. We are offering you the finest oak in Kent, come and see the trees for yourself."

"We will say six pieces." Mr Sutton drew a ledger towards him, and opened it.

"Six pieces! It costs us as much to bring the timber up to your door."

"Six pieces is my last offer." Sutton jotted some figures down on his tablets; he had become as remote and indifferent as a sultan, giving his orders to a slave.

"Very well," I bowed in resignation, though actually it was a whole piece more than we had expected to receive.

"I am sorry for my master, but you have always bought from us, and so this year we must make a sacrifice to meet your terms. Will it suit if we bring the timber up next Wednesday?" I looked out of the window and saw that it was already noon. It would be too late to ride to Kent until the following day.

"Wednesday...Wednesday...no, I have Sir Antony coming that morning about a farm that he wishes to sell. Suppose we say Thursday?"

"Agreed." I got up, and glanced again towards the arras. "I wish I could persuade my master to accompany the wagons, and see your treasures, but the good gentleman has lost all taste for travel."

"He is wise. I envy him for staying quietly on his land and not risking health and fortune in this corrupt City. And now, Sands, wait a moment and I will instruct my factor to give you ten pieces on account."

"Thank you, no." I shook my head. "My master knows you to be a man of your word, and he would not wish me to ride the highway alone, with gold in my wallet. When we bring up the three loads, I shall have four or five well-armed fellows with me, and we can carry the full sum back with us."

"My good friend Penny was always prudent, even as a boy. At least," he clapped his hands, "we must drink his health before you leave."

I sat down again in surprise. Usually Mr Sutton's factor had taken me to the kitchen, because the old, open hospitality of my boyhood was at an end, and a great merchant seldom drank with a man not of his own rank. "It will give you another five minutes with the arras," he said, smiling at my astonishment. "Country people have little liking for art, but Mr Penny told me, I believe, that you were born in London."

"I was. I happened to be passing when a thief attacked Mr Penny. I shouted for help, and he was kind enough afterwards to take me into his service."

"I like to see a man loyal to his master, it is rare nowadays."

I bowed. Sutton was making these remarks to pass the time, while the maid was putting a flagon of wine on the table; there was something very different on his mind, and I wondered what he could possibly want from me? Perhaps he wished to enquire about some gentleman in our neighbourhood who had come to him to borrow money? Or did he need some extra beams to make an alteration to his house? He waited until the maid had shut the door, and then said, raising his glass, "Have you ever thought, Sands, of doing business for yourself?"

"Business! The horse I ride belongs to my master, these clothes I wear are his gift. I have nothing in my pocket but my wages."

"I have a great respect for your master, Sands; when we

were boys in school together, I planned that we would work as partners, here in Cheapside. He was always wiser than I was," Sutton sighed, and looked at me as piously as if he were quoting from a sermon, "he preferred his apricot orchard to the burdens and disturbances of wealth. Yet now, who is his heir?"

The question was displeasing to me. I had earned my position as Mr Penny's clerk, through following a rule I had made during the early days of my service. Gossip was meat and drink to the small Kentish villages, but I had never discussed my master's affairs with either the timber men or his friends. "He lost his wife from a lingering fever many years ago," I answered cautiously, "we have all marvelled that he never remarried."

"I heard that his brother died last July."

"Yes," I nodded, "it saddened us all summer. The good gentleman was so much younger than my master, that he looked upon him almost as a son."

"So the nephew will inherit?" The maid had spread a little embroidered cloth in front of him, and Sutton's long fingers began to trace the pattern on it, as if the holes were zeros in a ledger. He seemed to be thinking something over, and to hesitate. Perhaps the enquiries were mere courtesy, and this was a signal to leave? I finished my wine, and pushed back my chair. "Do you know him?" The question came so sharply, and so suddenly, that I sat down again for the second time. "Why, no, the gentleman has been these two years at the Inns of Court, and though he came to us for the funeral, I did not see him afterwards. I had to go to Long Witherton. There was some story about vagabonds breaking into one of the barns."

"I have seen him," Sutton refilled the two glasses, "he borrowed the value of a farm from me to buy a collar of Venetian work for his new doublet. You can find him any afternoon at the *Dagger*, drinking wine, and playing tables with as lively a group of wastrels as any in England."

"His uncle would be much distressed to hear of the company he keeps," I said primly, because the *Dagger* was notorious both for high prices and doubtful manners. "Do you wish me to inform him?"

"No, Sands, it would be a waste of breath. The young fool would be haled home, but in less than a month, after some show of repentance and even some false tears, he would come back to his studies with more gold than ever in his pockets, and be even more gullible. There is no fool so stupid as your heir who thinks himself a lawyer because he has studied cozening at first hand, in some tavern."

I nodded again. I had seen enough of them in my Southwark days, and knew how such fellows had ended.

"What I want you to do is to serve both yourself and your master. If I do not break with London soon, the jade will have me by the throat until I die. To be plain, I want to buy Long Witherton."

"I fear my master would never sell the place. It was his father's land, and his grandfather's before him."

"And when he dies, his nephew will drink it up in half a year; in the best Canary, I grant you, he has a taste in wine. I saw that when he visited me. Surely it is better for Long Witherton to come to me," Sutton rapped the table impatiently, "than for a usurer to seize it, who does not know hay from beans?"

"You may command my services, Mr Sutton, but I fear lest you rate them too highly. How is a poor clerk to persuade his master to sell something almost as dear to him as his own life?"

"A direct report is no persuasion, it is your indirect attack that is deadly. There is much power in the single word, dropped in the right spot, at the right moment. I have seen three or four miserable syllables tumble a courtier from his palace chamber to the stinking hold of a leaky vessel where, poor fool, he hoped to mend his broken fortunes. And that is why I need you, Sands, you have your master's ear. Ride home with a troubled countenance, hang your head, and avow, if pressed, that you have heard it freely discussed all over London that Sir Antony Middleman covets Long Witherton to enlarge his mansion. He hopes to entertain the King."

"It is true that we have heard even in the country that there was a project to add a timbered staircase to the Hall."

"Exactly, and Sir Antony, rich as he is, will have to do some borrowing in the City, before he can pay for the furnishings."

"My master will reply that he is an honest man, and that not even the King can oblige him to sell his inheritance against his will."

"My poor friend has lived so long among his beehives that his wits are addled. If Sir Antony covets Long Witherton, he will get it, whether the owner be an honest man or no."

"Forgive my ignorance, sir, but how could he do this? Surely an enforced sale would not be far from piracy."

"Piracy!" Sutton laughed until the tears came into his eyes. "Sands, you are more innocent than I thought. Dost suppose the Court is strange to it?"

I looked up in such astonishment that Sutton continued. "Long Witherton is near enough to the coast to be an excellent base for any cargo landed on your marshes; not that I think your master has any share in such a traffic," he added, as I started to interrupt him, "but it exists, you know, it exists."

"Our village is honest," I protested hotly, "besides, we are thirty miles from the sea. The ruffians stopped a fishing smack the other day, and took the catch, and they sank a barque, a few miles out of Dover. All that I have seen arrive on the beach were a few sailors who had got away in their little boat, the poor wretches hadn't a cloak between them."

"I suppose the fools who owned her had paid no ransom

money. Ah, well, Sands," he smiled again at me grimly, "we shall have pirates with us as long as certain friends of theirs have influence at Court."

"But the Government…" I began.

"I am afraid, Sands, that you have blunted your own tolerably good wits with that strong country beer."

"People do not know," I muttered. It could not be true, yet one incident after the other rushed into my mind, and fitted themselves together like panes into a casement. Of course our bailiff was an honest man, but why had he smiled at me when I had complimented him upon his wine? There had been a broken wagon wheel under the bracken that nobody could explain. And the Spanish knife that I had seen a shepherd carrying! The solid boards of the floor beneath me seemed to be rocking under my feet.

"No. There are probably a number of honest fools even among the noblemen who would be as startled as you seem, if they knew the facts. Nor do I like it any more than you do. If we tolerate piracy on the seas, why should we pay the Guard to drive robbers from the streets? I risk my ship to the mercy of the winds, and if she escapes the hazards of nature and man, a third of my gain goes to an upstart in Whitehall, who does not know the difference between a fore top and a mizzen. But life is what it is, not what it ought to be, so let us leave such dreams for meat to the preachers. I am not asking you to risk your neck. It would look well in time in a lace collar. I do not want to snatch your master's land unpaid from him, although I have no doubt that any cunning lawyer could find a fault in his title to it. No, Sands, in my way I am as honest as your master. I need Long Witherton, and Sir Antony cannot filch it from my hands, because he will have to come to me, for the cost of his gilding and his tapestry. I will pay my old schoolfellow more than a fair price, and if you do my bidding, you shall be my bailiff there. Why, if you serve me as well as you have served him, in a few years you will be able to buy a holding of your own, because I never mind putting an opportunity in the way of an honest servant. So you see, I am not asking you to be disloyal, but only to be reasonable."

"I will do everything I can," I answered with apparent gratitude. If I refused, Mr Sutton would begin some other, even more dangerous trick. It was better to appear to agree, and then report on my return, all or some of the conversation to my master.

"Say nothing as yet to him about the nephew. Your first task is to persuade Mr Penny to come up himself with the oak. By the time that my lawyer and myself have finished talking to him, he will be so bewildered that he will beg us to take the farm, rather than have Sir Antony cozen it out of his hands. But have no fear, Sands, he shall have a fair price for it."

"I have known you long enough, sir, to be sure that you

will deal with him honestly." I got up, and this time Sutton
made no effort to detain me, but rose himself. "What are
you going to do with the rest of the day?" he asked curiously. "If you want advancement, you must not bury yourself
the year round in a village. The country is healthy enough
for a few months, now and then, but a man must keep in
touch with the times, even, if you will let me say so, with
the fashions. Your doublet is a good cut but it should be
three inches longer, and the sleeves should be much wider.
What about a play this evening at Blackfriars? I was there
the other night, and a witty fellow, Mr Robinson, acted the
dolt who is cheated of his daughter's dowry by a penniless
suitor so perfectly that I forgot that it was counterfeit. He
was the voice and form of old Alderman Bennett, that tire-
some fool from the Drapers' Company, the one who would
speak at all the pageants; he died last year. Why, when Mr
Robinson came skipping down the stage with thin legs, under a fur-trimmed mantle, fingering a great, gilt chain and
saying *welcome, to our great city of Luddong,'* and he pro-
nounced it Lud-dong, just like old Bennett, I laughed till I
cried. Robinson is not just a player. They say he has a fine
house, with as good a collection of Italian paintings as any
nobleman at Court. But no, Sands," he smiled, for in spite
of myself I had started at the mention of Dicky's name,
"plays are not for you. Confess that your vice is a sermon,
you would rather go to Paul's."

"You misjudge me," I answered in mock anger, "I am no friend of preachers, except at the prescribed times of service."

"You are right, they never helped a man yet, as far as I could judge. Well, you are modest, but I shall know your desires in time, and believe me, Sands, I shall help you to them within reason. And now, Mr Scrivener is waiting for you downstairs, together with a good roast capon and some wine. It may be better that you do not come up with your master next week. I leave that to your judgement. I am sure that I can leave this little matter," he added with a flattering smile, "completely in your hands."

A rather untidy maid put a great platter of roast chicken on the table, and a boy followed her with a small piece of beef. Scrivener, Sutton's London factor, got up to carve; in his black suit with the plain, white bands, he might have been mistaken for a Puritan. We were alone in a small room that once must have formed part of the kitchen, and here, at the back of the house, looking out on a courtyard, it was as quiet as a country manor.

I was glad not to have to eat at an ordinary, because eight years of farmhouse cooking had spoiled me for the stale food that was served in the taverns. The meat was tender, the chicken well larded with bacon, and Scrivener had filled my plate up with the best pieces, yet my conscience pricked me as I began; when I had taken leave from Mr Sutton I ought to have ridden immediately to my master. I should have had to abandon the walk that I had promised myself through the haunts of my boyhood, and it would have been too late to reach the village before nightfall, but had I hurried, I could have slept at the miserably uncomfortable inn halfway on the main road and been at home by mid-morning. Oh, there were excuses enough, I had had a long walk on little breakfast, and what man has a clear head on an empty stomach? There was the news of the town to hear, another merchant to visit, but I was uneasy all the same, and Mr Scrivener noticed my silence, because he said sharply, "Six pieces is an excellent price; if my master has a fault, it is that of lavishness!"

"Everything costs so much, especially rope."

"Agreed!" (He used the word in the same way, and with the same intonation as the merchant.) "There is also too much discontent."

"Mr Sutton sets a good table for his guests," I said politely, because I did not want to be drawn into any argument. I was glad that I had remembered to use the right title, for master was becoming a country term. "I had not expected him to bid me stay for dinner."

"It is not our custom to allow a client to go away unfed," the factor said reprovingly. This was untrue; on previous occasions I had been given grudgingly a small glass of wine to swallow as hastily as possible. "You must not wait on me," he added, as I looked across at his plate; he had taken only a small fragment of the wing. "I am never hungry, I suppose it is this stale London air."

"Air is the only advantage that we country people have over you," I answered humbly. "Mr Sutton must have thought me a veritable bumpkin this morning, I could not take my eyes from his arras." I hoped by praising something in the house to ease Scrivener's irritation. I suspected that he regarded me as an intruder.

"Do you like it?" he answered indifferently. "I would sooner have bare boards myself, these hangings are mere flea traps."

"To us, it is a spectacle. We see nothing but bare, brown furrows between Michaelmas and Easter."

"There are enough shows in our streets, if you will, but what does a wise man need for honest recreation other than a friend, and some wine?"

"And reasonable talk. I hear arguments about the price of pea sticks, and nothing else, from one evening's end to the other."

"I think Mr Sutton mentioned that you were London bred?" Scrivener looked at me searchingly, as if trying to recall some occasion when he might have met me.

"I come from Southwark, if you call that London."

"It depends what part," he answered with an unpleasant smile, and I knew that he was alluding to the roistering houses along the river. Then he added quickly, in case I was offended, "I suppose it was all country when you were a boy?"

"Yes, some of it was, and I was born in what was practically a hamlet in the marshes. After my parents died, I worked as stableman for an innkeeper, but alas, the good man died." I was altering the facts a little, while keeping as closely to the true story as seemed prudent; after I had left, I knew that Scrivener would report on me to Mr Sutton. Poor Humphries, I thought, as I sipped my wine slowly, I missed him more every year. It must have been five summers now since the carrier had brought me news of his death, but at least he had had the satisfaction of seeing me honestly settled in Kent before he died, and during the last winter of his life he had had fires enough to keep him warm, for I had earned enough by then to send him a load of faggots.

"Then Fortune, I see, has been kind to you." I felt the factor's eyes appraising the cloth of my doublet, and noting that it was of excellent quality in spite of a somewhat old-fashioned cut. "I was a mercer's apprentice myself, until Mr Sutton took me into his service."

"We have both been lucky in our masters," and I raised my glass solemnly.

"Sometimes they are grateful for our services. More often they are, like princes, inconstant in their favours." Scrivener's eyes caught mine, and I started; I had never seen such malevolence in any man's face.

"Not Mr Sutton," I said with apparent conviction, "he is a gentleman of his word."

"Oh, I was speaking of men in general," the factor said hastily, "still, if you had the riff-raff of this City to deal with, as I have, you would be thankful for your bare furrows and dreamless nights. There's a clerk, as you or I might be, trusted with his master's secrets, even with his money, and after a lifetime of toil and prudence, what happens to him! His master dies, forgetting him in his will, and the heir has his own servants or has mortgaged the property already to a usurer, so the poor wretch, after he has pawned his broadcloth suit, comes and begs me to let him sweep the yard for a penny."

"People seem more harsh than in my youth."

"Or else a man grows old. He has experience, he knows when to sell and when to wait for the prices to rise again, but because he walks a little stiffly, or does not present himself so well as some young upstart with a new turn of speech that has caught his master's fancy, he is turned away or sent to some wretched village to look after the second daughter's dowry or the gentleman's widowed mother."

I nodded. Much the same thoughts had been spinning through my head, since my interview with Sutton. Penny was an elderly man, and the loss of Long Witherton would break his heart. If the nephew were as wild, and deeply in debt as was said, my days in Kent were numbered. In the eyes of the village, I was only a foreigner. I could sell timber, they agreed, but I could not fell it, and because I had watched over my master's interests, any petty resentments they might feel about the strictness with which I kept the tallies fell on my head and not on his. I should not find it easy, either, to obtain other employment. "As long as we are mortal, we shall fear," I murmured.

Scrivener stared at me a moment, then he decided that I was quoting from a sermon. "These days a man must look after himself," he muttered morosely, and filled up our glasses.

The woman came in with a great cheese, and took away our plates. Scrivener passed it over to me, but when he helped himself, cut barely enough to cover a crust of bread. "And what is the news in town?" I asked, because I could not leave abruptly, and I hoped if he talked, it would ease his ill temper.

"News!" He shrugged his shoulders. "The same that there always is. A courtier used to appear in a fresh suit once a season, and now the fashion in doublets changes every week. Good for the mercers, and excellent for dealers in land. There were a dozen robberies last night, and as many brawls. They say that a man was killed at the *Dagger*, and if you were likely to frequent such taverns, I should warn you to be careful, but I see that you are as sober in your tastes as I am."

"Was it a quarrel?"

"Who knows? So as not to be charged, they threw the

body into the street where the Guard found it, but it was not far from their door."

"That is why my master refuses to come to London. He says that it has grown too dangerous."

"Mr Penny is unlikely to go to such a place as the *Dagger*." Scrivener leaned back, and wiped his lips. He was staring at me so hard that I almost choked over a crumb of bread. Could it be that he feared that I might supplant him in Mr Sutton's favour? Did he want the factorship of Long Witherton for himself? The thought was so fantastic that I almost laughed aloud. Yet I could not help noticing the hatred in his voice as he continued, "I suppose your master has made it worth your while to stay mewed up with him in the country?"

"I cannot complain," I answered modestly. I had told Sutton the truth. I had nothing but my wages, but it might be safer to let them suppose that I had some other resources. "Still, Mr Penny keeps a tight hand over the accounts."

"He should," Scrivener nodded approvingly, "there is more chance then of advancement. Like master, like man, as they say." He laughed most disagreeably. "I hate your clap-a-glass-of-wine-in-front-of-everybody traders."

The maid dropped a pan, and the scolding voice of the cook rose from the kitchen. Scrivener sipped the last drops of his wine, with a dry intensity that reminded me of the moralities that I had played in as a child; the man was

Avarice itself. "I must pray you to excuse me now," I said, "I have a couple of errands to attend to, and wish to be at my lodging before sunset."

"If you are staying at your usual inn at Southwark, it is not a walk I should recommend you after dusk."

"'Tis a poor place, I know, but the stableman is honest, and besides, I must fit my entertainment to my purse." There were strangers at the *Plough,* but I had found a man who had once worked with Humphries; he kept a small inn nearer the main road.

"One glass more for the journey?" Scrivener lifted the bottle that had come from Sutton's cellar, and not his own, but I shook my head. "I am not used to such abundant cheer," I protested, "and I have a long ride in front of me tomorrow."

"Then we shall expect you on Thursday." He rose, rather too quickly. "Remember, Master Sands, conditions change quickly, and if a small but honest deal comes your way, I should be happy to assist you. Sometimes a great opportunity is lost for want of a few angels." He lingered over the last word, as if it had been the name of his love.

He knows, I thought; he is testing me to see if I will be an accomplice in the smuggling. If so, and I am willing to share my plunder with him, he will make a favourable report to his master. "I hope I may be of service to you," I bowed as ceremoniously as if I had been taking leave of Mr

Sutton himself, "this has been a memorable occasion for me, and I thank you with all my heart, for your hospitality and advice."

It was three o'clock. I was angry with myself for having dallied so long over the meal. I must reach Southwark before dusk, and I had still some business and a long walk in front of me. At this hour the streets were crowded with apprentices and servingmen, hurrying upon errands. Once or twice a man almost knocked me into the gutter, because I was so confused that I hardly noticed where I was going. I had always prided myself upon my ability to sift truth from fable, but what was fact, and what deceit, in the stories that Sutton and his man had told me? I tramped along, trying to recall my meetings with Mr Penny's nephew. The fellow had made little impression upon me, one way or the other, but I had not seen him more than a dozen times, and there had been the inevitable gulf between a gentleman's son and myself. Was he really this spendthrift, or just a youth making the most of a year's freedom before he settled down? What could I do, if he were gambling away his lands? Even if Mr Penny believed me, and fetched the young man home, he would hate me for the rest of his life, and my master was ailing, and growing old. As for the pirates, the more that I turned Sutton's words over in my mind, the more certain I became that they were true. Young Greenford had plenty of money in his pockets, although he had no land. I had seen the squire wink when Mr Penny had commended the wine, "it depends upon your vintner, not the vintage," and there had been a day when I ought to have ridden to the black-smith, but my horse had been found lame, for no apparent reason. Yet how was I to explain the situation to my master? To him, a lie was a lie, a judge was an incorruptible officer of the law; to suspect the Court of complicity was madness or treason. He might fly into a rage and go straight to Sir Antony, and then we should end in gaol. They would never leave a man at large who knew too much, and could not be trusted to keep his mouth shut. Yes, if I were clumsy, Long Witherton would be lost and Mr Penny would never get a gold piece for it. Yet what were we to do? "Times change," I muttered as I paced along, but my master was rooted in the past, and whatever happened in this chaos whirling round us, the loser was likely to be myself.

The buildings in Cripplegate were unaltered, but other-wise it was a different street. The bright, clear colours of Eliz-abeth's day were gone with their wearers. Everything was dark and soft, the hated Spanish influence was as apparent here as at Court. These fine, discreet velvets suggested candlelight and conference, the open air of bowling greens would ruin them, these silver laces would tarnish in rain. I stopped under Master Wilson's sign; it had been re-gilded, and seemed out of place among the other weathered emblems, hanging like a popinjay, until the winter storms washed off some of the newness. It made me feel old. I recognised the long crack under the casement, but the faces of the apprentices were strange, and the man who was holding up a roll of sorrel-coloured silk for a customer to appraise must be Wilson's grandson. I stood and stared, the days when I had run here for a ribbon were still fresh at my shoulders, yet, the instant afterwards, I thought of my present home, of how I would ride into the courtyard on the morrow and warm myself at our chimney corner. Where are the middle years, I wondered, what happened to them? Time tangled; it never ran in a straight scythe cut, as they pretended in the moralities, but lay in loops, like the grass at haying time when the conies scampered for safety, and stem and flower were upside down together.

Mr Penny had told me to enquire about some broadcloth, but I saw that he would do better in our own country town; the London materials were designed to set off lace or lawn, and were much lighter in weight than those he commonly used. I hesitated, anxious for memory's sake to enter a final time, when I heard young Wilson say, in a mannered voice that would have earned him a box on the ear from his grandfather, "Our factor from Ragusa will be here tomorrow, he is even now at the docks, watching them unload the bales."

"I thank you heartily, I will return in a day or so," the gentleman answered. His back was turned towards me, yet the figure seemed familiar, then I noticed that he was wearing the double of Mr Sutton's suit, except that it had a narrower, less extravagant collar. He swung round so suddenly, as I was about to go inside, that we almost bumped into one another in the doorway. "Why, Dicky," I exclaimed. "Mr Robinson."

Dicky looked up in surprise, he did not remember me. "Give you good day, sir," he began, in the cold and wary tone of a man who was used to dodging strangers.

"It is so long since we ate Mother Crofton's pies together, that I am not surprised you have forgotten me."

"James!" (Nobody but Dicky had ever called me James.) "Where hast thou been all these years? How dost thou?" We looked at each other, and I saw our old garret again, with Dicky sitting on a tattered cushion, his legs stretched out in front of him, acting out, with myself for audience, a device that he had just invented to procure a summer doublet for his Sunday walks.

"Well," I said proudly, because the last time that he had seen me, I had been almost in rags, "well, but no longer a player."

I saw his gaze go from the rim of my hat to the top of my good leather riding boots, and he smiled. "So I see ... so I see. Thou art fat, James, as fat as an alderman. Thou hast lined thy belly well, whatever else has happened to thee. Hast thou a shop in the City?"

"No, not a shop. I became the factor of a timber merchant in Kent."

"Thou dissembler!" He slapped me on the shoulder. "Verily, when I told our fellows that there was something working inside that quiet pate of thine, I divined better than I knew. They thought that thou wast stupid."

"I have been very lucky," I murmured modestly.

"And hast thou seen my play? Tell me, what didst thou think of it? We have come a long way from those brawling matches on an open stage."

"It grieves me, Mr Robinson, but till last night, I have not been in London for a year. I have to pay for this," and I touched my cloak, "with exile."

"Mr Robinson! To thee, I am always Dicky, James; when canst thou come and see my house? Thou hadst a pretty taste in pictures, I remember, and I have some portraits much commended by gentlemen of the Court, who are lately come from Italy. Not this afternoon, because we are rehearsing a new comedy. Oh, thou must contrive to be in London when we play it, it's the wittiest thing, very droll, and I have devised a new way with the candles..."

"Alas, I am compelled to go to Kent tomorrow, but only for a few days. I return next week and then, if I may, I shall wait on you. It will lighten my increasing age to gossip about our early follies."

"Age, why, James, thou art not above seven years older than I am!" I started because there were only three years actually between us, but Dicky continued, "Thou hast forsaken us too long, or thou wouldst not talk so foolishly. Though thou hadst some love for the countryside even then..." he smiled as if one memory after the other were floating through his mind, in the way the barges pass the Sovereign during a Whitsun river pageant, "I remember following thee miles along the Thames to see a swan's nest that existed only in thine own imagination."

"And how Master Taylor scolded us afterwards for being late for supper!" I could see Dicky now, standing beside the empty table, and murmuring dolefully, as he looked at his muddy boots, "It isn't as if I even *liked* cygnets!" We both laughed, and then our laughter died away; what had swans' nests and raisin pies to do with grown men? That lace at Dicky's throat came directly from the membership that should have been mine, yet now, after a dozen years, I felt further from the truth than ever. He might have been as innocent of my dismissal as a babe, or have contrived it with all the subtlety of the Duke of Cyprus negotiating a Venetian treaty. "I must be on my way," I sighed, "but today will be a festival for me. We have met again."

"Go to, James," but I could see that the compliment pleased him, "the next time we must dine together, quietly, at my house. I have a Ganymede brought from Florence that Mr Hilliard, the painter, has much commended. It has a rare beauty. The boy is looking up at the eagle without a trace of fright; you would say that he was some child, innocently watching a falcon." He lifted his hat graciously, as if we were still equals, and hurried, with a fencer's delicate step, across the street.

"May the Muses protect you in a cold and dreary world," I murmured, because the old admiration returned, and I might never have spent nights upbraiding him, in my head, for being a cruel and shifty knave. Yes, if he had turned now, and asked me for my savings to buy him a tinsel knot, I would have poured them into his hands. "Oh, Dicky," I continued in my thoughts, "you sent me to a kind of death, and yet you have the loyalty unasked, that Sutton wants to buy, and I refuse to sell." *Pray you be merry,* as the old song had it, this was a crazy world. "What d'ye lack," a prentice bawled in my ear, the passers-by began to look at me curiously, I should be late getting back to my inn. Yet the road was full of Dicky's presence, it made the silks shimmer more, it filled my head with echoes from our old tiring house, the air and the day had a silver of their own. It was not until I had turned the corner, and saw the Thames in front of me, that I remembered that he had never told me where he lived.

A sudden, unexpected sunlight outlined the trees, and the opposite Southwark marshes. The swamp with all its fevers on this "false spring" day was the mirror from which a haze rose to the misty, unimaginable colours of Prospero's words, as we had heard them at the Globe. It was the first time for many years that I had come back to this part of the river, and the landscape that I had once known inch by inch was at the same time familiar and incredibly strange.

The dark Thames (oh, here it was not silver) slipped easily below the wall on which I leant, a thread stringing London together from the quiet Fulham gardens to the palaces of the Strand. There was movement everywhere, it was the changing of the seasons, old wives hung up their last, end-of-summer washing, boys chopped wood, and beside me, on a wattle fence, I noticed a final, clinging rose. A prentice passed by whistling, as if, while the sun was out, he had nothing to do but forget his master and dawdle over his errand, as I had done myself, at his age, on a hundred occasions. Yet our brief July was over, we turned towards the cruel and bitter winter, when my attic was cold and lonely, and that despot, memory, plagued me with too many thoughts. I could hope for respite, an occasional small happiness, but I knew now that there would be no more magnificence; the game, as Mr Beaumont would have said, was almost over. It was less the grave that I feared than this slow, gradual extinction of all growth. We were doomed from birth, some to be fortunate, some otherwise; if certain seekers still called reason sweet, what was our real destiny but hazard?

Sands, you dreamer, changeling Sands, I heard the old

reproaches in the splashes of water falling from a waterman's oars, but on this late afternoon of what might be my last day in London (if Mr Penny's fortunes went as scurvily as I feared), nothing but imagination remained, or something so deep under it, that the bravest diver could not bring its name to the surface. "This is the answer," Ursula had said with her pretty assurance, one sunny afternoon. "Nobody will notice the stitch here but yourself. I can embroider the panel at my will, first the swans, and then the stars, or the other way about, but the design is known at the beginning, and it will be finished, though it may need a dozen hands to work on it. Or," she had added after a pause, "a dozen lives." Then we had both laughed, because we had listened to so much about Pythagoras in the library, that it was almost a joke. Yet who would want to buy my tapestry with all its rents and failures? Nature was prodigal with her roses, but my painful learning, my little victories, would pass in a second, and be less valuable than a leaf. I had sharpened my mind, only to sheathe it in myself.

On the other side of the river, two women were shaking a coat vigorously between them. At this distance, it was only a rag of scarlet, but because they were standing near the spot where I had lived, I felt suddenly unbelievably happy. I did not notice anything of youth, that had gone for ever, only a curious elation, a St Martin's summer of the blood, as if some long promised wish was about to be fulfilled. I thought of Awsten, and found in wonder that I could not remember his face, only far off the echo of his voice haunted the inner ear, but were the words his, or was it a phrase which had lost its validity through frequent repetition? Then as the skiffs passed, I began to see Martin in every one of the rowers, he was not my playfellow but a man, hailing me across the water, "Yes, Sands, it *was* always summer, why didst thou not come with me?" The cracked oar floating down the tide turned into a long island, rising from a blue, heraldic sea, and I hung over the parapet dreaming, forgetting dusk and its many dangers. I might have stayed there another hour, if someone had not kicked a pebble up behind me. "Good day, Master Sands, I have been following you for this half hour with a message."

"A message!" I turned to face a tall fellow, dressed in grey as soberly as myself, and with a sword at his side. I could not recall having seen him before.

"Yes, from Mr Scrivener. He told me that you were returning to your inn at Southwark, of which he did not know the name, and I lost you in this maze of alleys. Unless you had stopped to look at the river, I doubt if I should have caught up with you. It's a brave sight, the Thames...." He looked across at the wherries.

"Does Mr Scrivener wish to see me again?" I asked in surprise.

"No, if you will do me the honour to take a glass of

wine with me, he has given me authority to act for him. My name is Turner, and I am also in Mr Sutton's service."

"I will return," I said. I wanted to keep on good terms with the factor, and even if it meant an hour's delay it would be wiser to talk to the man himself than to discuss some possibly private matter with still another servitor.

"I fear Mr Scrivener is occupied. He would have followed you himself, but Mr Sutton sent for him, directly after your departure. It is a small matter, the question of some timber for a friend."

I hesitated; in spite of my suspicions the fellow looked honest enough, and no excuse came readily to my mind.

"Here is a token, Master Sands." Turner flashed a signet ring under my eyes, but returned it so quickly to his pouch that I could not be certain whether it had borne the Sutton arms or not. "There is a reasonably good tavern in the next street to this, and wine, they say, keeps the autumn chills from the bones."

"I want to reach my lodging before sunset," I said doubtfully; it would take me another half hour of brisk walking, to cross the bridge and get to my inn.

"I will not detain you five minutes, I promise you, but Mr Scrivener will be greatly disappointed if I return without your answer."

I bowed, and my companion turned briskly into a narrow lane that I had not previously noticed. We walked side by side without speaking, and I perceived with a growing uneasiness that though Westminster could not be far away, we were going deeper and deeper into such a labyrinth of alleys that I had lost my sense of direction. I suspected Scrivener both of knowing my plight and of wanting to make me some offer of help, probably through this man Turner, so that, at need, he could disclaim all knowledge of it afterwards. The factor might have decided that I could become a useful tool, or after my departure, Mr Sutton might have been frightened that I would blurt the truth out to Mr Penny. Whatever it was, any aid would have its price, and the further we went, the more I disliked the matter. "Where is this inn?" I enquired almost sharply. "It is getting late."

Turner pointed to a dusty sign. "Has the short cut confused you? The river is just behind us." He opened the door, but afterwards brushed past me with little ceremony, and to my surprise did not sit down in the main room which was empty, but led me instead down a passage into a small, dark chamber with a single table and some stools. "Nobody will disturb us here," he said, as he hung his cloak on a nail in the wall.

A drawer had shuffled after us with some wine, and it was evident from his greetings that Turner was well known in the tavern. He waited until the servant had left the room, before he picked up the sack. "To your health," he said, "do you often make this long journey to London?"

"Once a year." I tasted the wine, but it was the rough, heavy stuff that they kept for chance wayfarers. Turner emptied his own glass greedily, and looked at me with scorn. "Come," he encouraged, "drink up."

"You must excuse me," I protested, "I have many hours of riding in front of me tomorrow, and I am not as young as I was."

"Wine is the best medicine to make a man forget his age and the discomforts of the road." He poured himself another glass, and I emptied my own out of politeness.

"And now, this timber? Mr Scrivener wants to buy a separate load?" I enquired. The sour air, and the dirt, on top of the heavy dinner that I had had, were making me queasy.

"It is not really for himself, but for a friend. Between ourselves," Turner leaned across the table, and winked, "it is a private matter, not for his master's ears."

"We could bring a load up easily with the rest of the timber, but does he know a man to whom we could deliver it?" I was convinced that the story was simply an excuse, but I could not imagine what there might be behind it.

Instead of replying, Turner stared at me almost insolently. "You were born at Southwark, I believe; I think we have met at the *Angel?*"

"The *Angel!* I am a poor clerk, and that is far beyond my purse. Besides, I was a boy when I went into the country."

Turner nodded, there seemed to be something on his

mind. "What sour stuff this sack is," he grumbled, "it would be inhospitable to let you leave with such a taste in your mouth. Harry," he shouted, "art ready?" There were heavy steps outside, and a fellow entered in a stained leather jerkin. I saw in horror that he had lost his ears.

The man closed the door behind him. I started up, but it was too late. "There is a little matter to settle with you, Master Sands," Harry mocked, and I recognised an unpleasant, taunting voice that I had last heard on a certain stormy evening at the *Plough*. "Poor Noll, you did him a great unkindness, and you owe him some reward."

"Yes, we might be willing to let you go," Turner said, moving quickly to his companion's side, "if you hand us the gold Mr Sutton gave you this morning. It was ten pieces, I suppose; they will balance the sum that you saved your master on a former occasion. We shall require a little interest as well — news, say, as to when the worthy gentleman is expected to reach London."

"And something to compensate poor Noll for his branding, and the six months he languished in the *Counter*."

"I received nothing from Mr Sutton," I answered; "do you suppose that I am foolish enough in these times to ride alone to Kent with gold in my wallet? Here is all I have…" and I emptied my purse on to the table, a few sixpences, some farthings, and a round, half ryal.

"Is it not a sad thing that a poor man's life should depend

on riches? I am afraid that you may never see the Thames again without a proper ransom. A pity, because I noted that you were an admirer of its beauties. Still, you will find that we are less harsh than your aldermen; if your pockets are really as empty as they seem, we might let you go this once, but you must tell us first where young Greenford meets the London agent."

"Young Greenford! But I do not know the gentleman."

"Come, Sands, still so lily-livered? A friend of mine saw you conversing with him, very merrily, at the *Ship* last Sunday."

"Mr Greenford stopped at my table to ask me about some beams that he wanted to buy from my master. I have never exchanged a word with him otherwise."

"Make up your mind. Ten pieces of gold, or the name of the place where Greenford receives protection money for the safe conduct of certain vessels."

"I haven't the one, and I do not know the other."

"How sad! We shall have to treat you, then, as you treated our comrade." Turner kicked the table aside, and as the coins scattered over the floor, I had just time to draw my sword.

"He means to fight," Turner jeered, as Harry came towards me. If only I had practised my fence, but I had not had a blade in my hand these last six years! A point flashed, it was a long, evil-looking rapier, and I parried in tierce;

I was better that side. The fellow soon noticed this, and shifted to carte.

It was useless to shout for help, no constable could hear me through these dank, thick walls. The ruffler struck again, and I pressed the point aside, but my weight was against me, I could not get my breath. "Poor soul," I heard Turner's mocking voice from near the door, "the sands are running out. By your name you should be master of them, but what can you do to stay them?" and he laughed.

My limbs contracted into a cold and heavy terror. I had always been afraid of being trapped. "A moment," Turner said sharply, knocking up our blades with his sword.

"You see. Harry is the best swordsman ever to come out of Shoreditch. If you value that carcass of yours, tell us the name of the meeting place. We have other business on hand beside yourself."

I looked round the squalid room, at the dirty walls and the overturned furniture. "How can I tell you what I do not know?" I protested.

"In that case there is nothing to do, but to throw you into the Thames."

Then — it came to me in a flash — I knew that the place was Long Witherton. I had met Greenford in one of the lanes whenever I had ridden there, and a chance remark of the forester, during my last visit, came back into my head. "Old Mrs Bridger thinks she has seen a ghost. By the way that the bracken has been trampled down, there were six of them if you ask me, and there was nothing ghostly about them either, they were poachers." Sutton knew where these fellows met, and that was why he wanted to buy the estate. "It might be anywhere among the woods," I suggested, to gain time.

"Come now, we know that you have been to the place. If you are afraid of your master, we are taking care of that gentleman anyhow. If you are disturbed as to how to fill your belly, we might let you pick up a coin or two, if you make yourself agreeable."

"I should be a fool not to tell you if I knew," I said. "Let me return to Kent, and I will find out the name in a day."

"And call out the Guard! No, Sands, we are not as stupid as that. Either confess exactly where these fellows meet, or you have seen your last sunset on this or, to my mind, any other earth."

All was lost. If I told them they would still slit my throat; there was no escape for either my poor master or myself from this plot into which we had innocently stumbled. I should never know whether Sutton had mistrusted me, if Scrivener had bribed them so as to be rid of a possible rival, or whether Noll had noticed me entering the merchant's house that morning by pure chance. "I don't know," I cried out desperately; it was much less real than those parts that I had played as a youth, when kingdoms had crumbled and emperors had died in the brief space of two hours. Only then we had got up, dusted off our clothes; if I had forgotten a line, somebody had given me a clout, but afterwards we had watched the moon rise, leaning out of our attic window, or Dicky had lain in his trundle bed and mocked the world, from the gutter to the Court.

Turner nodded. His companion sprang at my chest. I beat him back, but my arm was slow, my wrist was stiff. I know now, I thought, my duty was to stay with Martin, dying would have been easier beside some soft and lazy sea. "He is tiring," a voice sneered, "hurry, there is too much noise." I parried the strokes, but aimlessly, because all I could see were rings of steel. They would throw my body into the river, and nobody would know what had become of me. Sands... little James Sands... the apprentice Sands... pity and tenderness and wonder, all were ending; the room filled with the heavy, earth-like scents of a wood of wild daffodils, my failures spread out in front of me, the missed opportunities were clearer than my opponent's face. Things change, there is no part for you in the next play, everything has its end. How stupid, I almost muttered, I haven't finished yet. The point nearly caught my arm, but I pressed it back. Long Witherton, what did it matter whether I screamed the name or not? Yet there seemed some reason why I should go to my grave without saying it. Then my head cleared; yes, when I did not return, Mr Penny would ride over to Sir Antony, and even if he had to sell the farm, they were neighbours, and my master's life and the rest of his property would be safe.

My back was against the wall, I could retreat no further, it was the final moment of not breathing that I feared. I want to see Sundridge again, I thought, and remember the voices; let me have one more April. In a wild fury that I had been trapped like any country fool, I lunged forward. I just saw Turner leap, the flash of his rapier aimed at my throat, as Harry stepped backwards; then the world crashed into a great sea, into such pain that everything spun into a bright, high silence....

I knew that I was dead.

Afterword

RYHER WROTE the following letter to her friend, the scholar and editor Norman Holmes Pearson, in response to questions about her fascination with the Elizabethan era. We include it here as a wonderful closure to the publication of the Paris Press edition of the novel. We hope that by offering Bryher's own explanation of why this period was essential to her, readers will come to understand what propelled her to write the story of James Sands.

Paris Press has made typographical corrections in the letter, which Bryher herself noted on the original typed pages; we have corrected several additional misspellings and in a few instances we have regularized the punctuation. Paris Press thanks the Estate of W. Bryher and the Beinecke Rare Book and Manuscript Library at Yale University for permission to reproduce this epistolary epilogue.

⸰⸰∽ᘓᖇᘍ∽⸰⸰

VILLA KENWIN
BURIER S/LA TOUR
VEVEY
TÉLÉPHONE: BURIER 5.29.27

14th January 1953

My dear Norman,

When did I learn to read Elizabethan? It would take pages
to tell you. I can give you the exact date, on my seventh
birthday I was given a volume of *Tales from Shakespeare*,
not Lamb's edition but a version by E. Nesbit. From that
moment I was lost to their enchantment. I read, at that age,
only for the stories, and I remember particularly Imogen
finding the cave on the hillside, Pericles picking up the suit
of armor from the beach and Ferdinand and Miranda playing chess. One day, the impression was so vivid that looking
up from the London balcony where I was sitting, the rail-
ings round the square turned into rushes and I saw Imogen

and some other characters from the plays, moving among the trees, or if you will, in Arden.

The things we know first remain with us longest. Shakespeare was the background to my earliest impressions, and when I was about eleven, my Mother gave me a one volume edition of the plays. I read them mixed up with boy adventure books, and naturally picked out the battle scenes. They were there, something to be known, and though I do not remember learning any of the poetry then by heart, the names and the places became constantly more familiar.

My next Elizabethan venture happened when I was fifteen. I wanted to draw animals and found a place where an unwilling or reluctant horse or dog was bribed to stand on a platform, while a strange assembly of a few children and some elderly owners of pets sat round it and sketched most earnestly with charcoal. For six weeks I was completely happy. Strange as it might sound, it was to me the veritable "school of Epicurus." About the same time, scrambling along the ledge of a bookshelf in my Father's library, I discovered Hazlitt's *Dramatic Literature of the Age of Elizabeth.* (I have been glad to think subsequently that Hazlitt passed much of his childhood in the States.) Besides introducing me to many authors of whom I had never heard, there was one of Bellario's speeches. A few days later I found Lamb's *Specimens of Dramatic Poetry* with a whole scene from *Philaster*. But the catch was that I became suddenly so absorbed with poetry and art, with lines and shapes and sounds, that I forgot to answer "yes" and "no" at the right moment. It shocked the adult world and I found myself transferred over night to a large boarding school, in order that I might learn to be "like other people." Having been brought up mainly abroad, I was completely unprepared for the experience. I knew nothing of the slang, customs nor habits of thought among my contemporaries. In all good faith, I interviewed the head mistress during the first week that I was there, with a project to re-organise service at meals to obtain not only greater comfort but more efficiency, and to demand an enquiry into our history lessons, I had been deeply shocked to find that nobody in my class was aware of the immense gulf between chain mail and plate armor. I was promptly turned out of the history class, as knowing more history than was "good for me," but the school had its revenge with maths. Although subsequently I was able to cope with three rates of foreign exchange going on at the same time, ciphers were a blank to me. I regret this, because I should like to understand aerodynamics and though I have a book on the subject, written for children of ten, I stick at the first chapter because of my inability to comprehend the simplest formula. I like to think this is due to the way that we were taught, but I have an ominous suspicion it is my own stupidity.

School was, however, a grimly unhappy time, how un-happy I only realised many years later. You will remember the apartment where we lived in London during the last war and I know that you saw "our bomb crater" in the street below us. When that bomb fell we were lying on the floor and the walls rushed towards us and bent over. I did not see my past life flash in front of me, as one is supposed to do on such occasions, but I had time for two thoughts, "whatever this is, it isn't as bad as school," and "I wish I had seen New York in spring." Then, because they were concrete and not brick, the walls receded somehow into their proper positions, we got up, brushed away some of the dust, and made ourselves the inevitable cup of tea.

To return to my school days, however, Bellario seemed, not myself but someone who had the imagination and the courage that I too often lacked. Only my Philaster was art. And why Bellario, you will ask, why not Rosalind or Viola? Well, this was the overlapping of the Victorian with the Edwardian age and it was not a good time to be a girl. We were there to be "seen and not heard" and every good thing in life was reserved to boys. I wanted comparatively simple things but I wanted them badly. I should have liked to be a sailor and fight my way around the Horn, I felt the excitement in trade, as some of the Elizabethan merchants must have felt it, and organisation was a game to me. I frequently worked out how things could be improved so that they ran more smoothly, the school, travelling and so on, but nobody ever listened to me. I was a girl and girls did not go into business, did not climb masts, did not, above all, did not fight.

Rosalind fell in love, Viola was frightened of her sword but Bellario faced adventure and had the virtue that I valued then, more than any other, she was loyal. I was also much helped by the lines that Beaumont and Fletcher wrote on melancholy; I remember I declaimed these on the games field with much fervor and with correctly folded arms, you will know them, I think,

"Hence all the vain delights" etc.

So I read every Elizabethan play I could find but there were few reprints at that time and I began my serious study only about five years later, when my Father was persuaded to give me Dyce's edition of several Elizabethan dramatists. These were costly according to the values of that time, though only a fraction of what the price would be now. By then I was over the romances and it was not Bellario, but Roaring Moll who became my heroine. I hurried over the tragedies, what I wanted was the lusty, violent photographs of the age that Dekker and Middleton gave us in the comedies, because I needed to know how people acted in everyday life, what they ate, how they drew their swords, what they shouted at one another. One good thing was that my edition of the plays had few notes. I had to try and puzzle out the expressions for myself. Then, very solemnly,

I have never managed to be quite so serious again, I did my first piece of research, into the treatment of women in the Elizabethan age and having read a hundred and fifteen plays (and I assure you that I counted them) and having breathed, thought and listened to Elizabethan until I could hear no other language, my article on "The Girl Page in Elizabethan Literature" was published in the *Fortnightly Review*, and I even got twenty pounds for it. It was a deplorable performance, wrong from the first line to the last, but at least it was training.

Elizabethan had been my refuge during the horrible period of the first world war, a moment of history far worse to me and I think to most survivors from it, than the second war ever was, and it was natural that, after the war ended, I should drop Elizabethan for twenty years. I had other things to do. From 1932 I watched the second war coming and the more that I warned people, the more they laughed at me. I came back to England on the last day of September 1940, after an extremely difficult journey from Switzerland over Lisbon to London. A day or so later I was walking down towards Berkeley Square one afternoon, when a wall that had been undermined by a bomb, collapsed over the pavement just in front of me. I flew into a towering rage, because it was one thing to be heroically bombed and another, to have the anti climax of bricks almost killing one on a quiet afternoon. I think it was that evening or a day or two later that I picked up instinctively my Mermaid edition of Beaumont and Fletcher and re-read *The Knight of the Burning Pestle.*

There it was, that London of 1940, better than anything that you will find in any contemporary document. Good humor, stupidity, a sublime courage with at the same time, no understanding of what it was all about, substitute home guard for trained bands, and the picture is there before you. With my European training, I thought that the Germans probably would land, I had no longer the confidence of the nine year old, that "by pike and dyke" we should hold off an invasion, and so I suppose I must have re-read the play about fifty times during the subsequent six months.

So I was lost again, you see, but this time, besides the plays, I read all the histories, records and diaries that I could find. Alter the date from 1938 to 1613 or 1618, Munich and appeasement are the story of Ralegh over again. The best study of a pathological desire for "peace at any price" is to be found in the policies of James. That led, in great measure, to the English Civil War, a far more cruel affair than most people suppose. If something happened in our own world war two, I did not look at contemporary reports, I turned back first and studied it in the light of seventeenth century documents and reflected that the snail was too swift to be the emblem of Progress.

On Sunday mornings, when there was no traffic in the City, I went exploring Southwark or Aldermanbury, where Shakespeare, Hemminges and Condell once lived, or Cripplegate where they say, Armin was buried. The bell that rang out for Agincourt was destroyed in a big raid, I may have walked over its dust. These excursions gave me an illusion of being alive. In my spare time, which was very, very little, I must have taken out most of the books in the London Library on the Elizabethan and early Jacobite ages, with the exception of criticism of the plays. I was interested in the time, not simply the dramas. One afternoon I discovered Baldwin's *Organisation of the Shakespearian Company.* On page 278 occur the lines, "Sands, Phillips's apprentice, was to graduate about 1613." And on page 279, "Now as Euphrasia in *Philaster* (summer 1610) Sands had been 'about eighteen.'" From that moment on, the book wrote itself, although not at once. I was already in the middle of *The Fourteenth of October* and I knew that I did not dare to mix my periods. The actual writing may have taken three years because there was a couple of years after the war when I hardly wrote a line, but the preparation had been going on all my life. I do not pretend to have used every word as an Elizabethan might have spoken it, because my function is to relate past and present into a continuous whole, but I think the spirit is true enough to the times, it could have happened as it is presented.

And now — sources. No Elizabethan book to-day is respectable without them. I confess myself slightly amazed at the feverish search for a plot that bears some remote resemblance (as most plots do) to the particular author considered in a particular thesis. I am specially reminded of a learned author who devoted about fifty pages to a consideration of whether Shakespeare had influenced Beaumont and Fletcher or was it the other way around, because all the authors had used the words "dog" and "moon." No, the humblest, the least inspired author does not work that way. Inspiration comes from the air, a chance heard word, a forgotten memory some scent or color has suddenly recalled. But out of this cross-word puzzle aspect of modern research, the giants emerge. They leap through the to me so puzzling Elizabethan script as if it were headlines on a modern newspaper, they can give you the exact month when a word was first used, the hour that ash-color was no longer fashionable. To them, my infinite gratitude and thanks. I could not list all the books that have been as full of excitement to me as the adventure stories of my youth, but without the few I like to recall here, perhaps my Sands would never have been written: — all of Dr Hotson's books, Bakervill's *The Elizabethan Jig*, Baldwin's book mentioned above and his *Shakespeare's Petty School*, Prouty's *Gascoigne*, and Ralegh's *Poems* edited by Agnes Latham, together with her occasional studies. There is Rowse's *Elizabethan England and Tudor Cornwall*, books by Professor Neale, Sisson's *Lost Plays*, and an old book, Cohn's *Shakespeare in Germany*.

The fun has been being permitted to sit in the corner while the experts talk, and here I find it reasonable to be seen but not to utter. It has not always been strictly academic either. I recall the horror of a crowded tea shop when Miss Latham observed earnestly, "I am sure Sir Walter really loved his wife" and a circle of old ladies leaned forward, all ears, for the newest bit of scandal. Yes, that is the fun of "the game," the search, and the rare discovery. If we could turn time over and watch Drake return, it would be just another movie. It is the sifting, the hard work, and then, after twenty years the holding of one tiny fragment to fit to another piece as incomplete, to know that the solution of a problem may come only to the mind of somebody not yet born, that makes it all worth playing. I know so little and yet I can say I am an Elizabethan, because like them, the world itself interests me, flying and science and trade, as much as poetry and problems, and as I have said before, it is a whole and I cannot tell you where yesterday ends and to-day begins — I suspect that like them, I want only "to-morrow."

Bryher.

About Bryher

BRYHER was born in England in 1894, the daughter of Sir John Ellerman, a prominent industrialist and financier. Her early education was unconventional and highlighted by lengthy travels throughout France, Italy, and the Near East — an upbringing that awoke in her a lifelong passion for history, archeology, psychology, and travel. Her formal schooling began at fifteen, when she was sent away to boarding school; there she bridled at the routine, but found consolation in her discovery of the Elizabethan dramatists, whose plays she recited to herself on the hockey field. Her holidays were spent exploring Cornwall and the Scilly Islands, from which she was to take her name, Bryher.

The outbreak of World War I forced Bryher to give up the study of archeology, and she turned to writing. She had two marriages of convenience. The first was to a young American writer, Robert McAlmon, with whom she founded Contact Publishing. Through Contact, she financed and supported the publication of Ernest Hemingway's first collection of stories, Gertrude Stein's *The Making of Americans,* Dorothy

Richardson's novels, and the work of numerous modernist writers in Paris and the U.S. Her second marriage was to Kenneth Macpherson, a Scottish author and film critic with whom she produced films (including *Borderline,* starring Paul Robeson) and published *Close Up,* an influential journal devoted to the art and social impact of the cinema.

Bryher spent the 1920s and 1930s in Paris and Berlin, traveling with her longtime companion, the poet H.D., and establishing her home in Territet, Switzerland. Following her expulsion from Switzerland in 1940, she returned to England after several years spent assisting over one hundred German and Austrian refugees to safety. She lived through the Blitz in London with H.D., and returned to Switzerland following the war. The next three decades were filled with an outpouring of literary activity during which she wrote a dozen novels and three memoirs, including *The Heart to Artemis: A Writer's Memoirs,* which Paris Press has republished in conjunction with this volume.

Bryher died in 1983 at her home in Territet. Though her work has been out of print and mostly unknown for nearly thirty years, it has always commanded the interest of discerning readers who appreciate her historically accurate, lifelike evocations of the past, the echoes of history in our present time, as well as — in the words of Marianne Moore —"her undeceived eye for beauty and her passion for moral beauty."

About Paris Press

PARIS PRESS is a not-for-profit press publishing neglected or misrepresented work by ground-breaking women writers. Paris Press values literature that is daring in style and in its courage to speak truthfully about society, culture, history, and the human heart. To publish our books, Paris Press relies on support from organizations and individuals. Please help Paris Press keep the voices of essential women writers in print and known. All contributions are tax-deductible. To contact the Press, please send an e-mail to info@parispress.org or write to Paris Press, P. O. Box 487, Ashfield, MA 01330.

The text of this book is composed in Adobe Garamond.
Decorative elements from the 1600s include an
ornament from *Rule a Wife* by Fletcher & Beaumont, 1640,
courtesy of the Mortimer Rare Book Room, Smith College.
Text design and typesetting by Lisa Carta.
Cover design by Ivan Holmes Design and Lisa Carta.
Cover photograph by R. Allison Ryan, copyright © 2006.
Printed by Quebecor World.